100 Reasons to Celebrate

We invite you to join us in celebrating
Mills & Boon's centenary. Gerald Mills and
Charles Boon founded Mills & Boon Limited
in 1908 and opened offices in London's Covent
Garden. Since then, Mills & Boon has become
a hallmark for romantic fiction, recognised
around the world.

We're proud of our 100 years of publishing
excellence, which wouldn't have been achieved
without the loyalty and enthusiasm of our
authors and readers.

Thank you!

Each month throughout the year there will
be something new and exciting to mark the
centenary, so watch for your favourite authors,
captivating new stories, special limited
edition collections…and more!

Dear Reader

Since my early teens, Mills & Boon® romance novels have carried me to faraway places and allowed me to experience exotic locales, fantasy lifestyles, and to fall in love time and again.

I truly believe love is the greatest gift any of us ever give or receive. For a hundred years Mills & Boon has given this gift to their readers—me and you.

They've provided an escape—to get lost in romance and to have faith in love and life renewed.

In THE HEART SURGEON'S SECRET SON, Daniel's faith in love is shaken when he discovers his high-school sweetheart gave birth to his son and never told him. Daniel is a hero I immediately fell in love with. He's dedicated, honourable—and did I mention sexy? Kimberly loves him with all her heart, and makes the decisions she believes are right—but, like many of us, she makes mistakes that sometimes exact a high toll.

It's an honour to be included in Mills & Boon's centenary celebration, as an author and as a lover of romance. Happy 100th Birthday!

I love to hear from readers. Please e-mail me at Janice@janicelynn.net, write to me care of Mills & Boon, or visit me at my website www.janicelynn.net

Janice

THE HEART SURGEON'S SECRET SON

BY
JANICE LYNN

MILLS & BOON®
Pure reading pleasure

All the characters in this book have no existence outside the imagination
of the author, and have no relation whatsoever to anyone bearing the
same name or names. They are not even distantly inspired by any
individual known or unknown to the author, and all the incidents are
pure invention.

First published in Great Britain 2007
Harlequin Mills & Boon Limited,
Eton House, 18-24 Paradise Road, Richmond, Surrey TW9 1SR

© Janice Lynn 2007

ISBN: 978 0 263 86306 2

Set in Times Roman 10½ on 12¾ pt
03-0208-42694

Printed and bound in Spain
by Litografia Rosés, S.A., Barcelona

Janice Lynn has a Masters in Nursing from Vanderbilt University, and works as a nurse practitioner in a family practice. She lives in the southern United States with her husband, their four children, their Jack Russell—appropriately named Trouble—and a lot of unnamed dust bunnies that have moved in since she started her writing career. To find out more about Janice and her writing, visit www.janicelynn.com

Recent titles by the same author:

THE DOCTOR'S PREGNANCY BOMBSHELL

CHAPTER ONE

Nurse Kimberly Brookes stared out her hotel window and, despite the room's warmth, shivered at the wintry blur of white obscuring Boston's skyline.

Or maybe the thought of having to spend the next week with Dr. Daniel Travis had triggered the goose bumps prickling her skin.

Either way, she felt chilled to the bone.

Within the hour she would come face-to-face with the one man she measured all others by. No one even came close to touching her heart the way Daniel did.

Was that why the thought of seeing him made her blood race and her hands shake?

As one of Cardico's key marketing sales executives, she needed to learn everything about the innovative pacemaker Daniel had helped to develop. Each sales executive would spend a week with Daniel, shadowing him, so they would have a full understanding of the life-saving device.

She'd delayed as long as she could. Now she prepared to face a man she'd once loved, a man she'd planned to never see again.

Who was she kidding?

There was no way to prepare for Dr. Daniel Travis. He'd done miraculous things to hearts long before he'd earned his medical degree, and she'd never been impervious to his allure.

Perhaps deep down she'd always known her path would cross Daniel's again.

She needed to get over her silly schoolgirl fantasies, and seeing him provided the only way to do that.

Hopefully, she'd see him and realize her youthful hormones had tricked her mind. No man could be as charismatic as she remembered Daniel.

Then again, wasn't she reminded daily just how charismatic he'd been? Just how blue those penetrating eyes had been?

Need squeezed her heart, and she glanced at her watch. Ryan would be awake. She picked up her cell phone and hit autodial to call her son's cell phone.

"Hey, Mom," he answered on the second ring. "I'm up and ready for school, if that's what you're wondering."

Just hearing his deepening voice caused her to smile. He hadn't expected the morning call. She'd called last night after she'd arrived at her hotel. She'd wanted to make sure he'd settled in at his best friend Tyler's house for the week. Kimberly and Tyler's mother, Beth, had gotten to be good friends over the years, and the boys often stayed over at each other's homes.

"I never thought otherwise," she admitted. Ryan was a good kid, an honor student and a star athlete. Like his father, he excelled at almost everything he attempted. When he did run across a new challenge, he stuck it out until he mastered yet another skill.

She'd always encouraged him to try new things, to be well rounded and to chase his dreams. It's what a loving mother did. Hadn't she experienced firsthand the lengths a mother would go to to protect her child?

Ryan was her whole world. They'd gone through life's journey alone for so long, just the two of them. And, despite everything, they'd done all right.

Better than all right.

Her eyes watered and she swiped at them. She was being ridiculously sentimental and knew the cause.

"I just called to say I missed you," she said into the phone, trying to hide her emotional state, "and hope you have a good day at school."

"Aw, Mom," he said, but she could hear the pleased teasing in his voice. They'd always been close, and thus far Ryan hadn't shunned her affectionate nature. "I told you that you should have brought me."

"Missing school for a week was not an option," she reminded him, knowing academics played the least role of why she'd refused to consider Ryan coming with her to Boston.

"Yeah, yeah, but think how educational the trip would have been for me to visit Paul Revere's house and the site of the Boston Tea Party and the—"

"Nice try," she interrupted. "Maybe next time."

A time when she wouldn't be spending every moment in Daniel Travis's company.

Someone spoke to Ryan in the background.

"Hey, Tyler's mom is ready to leave for school," Ryan said. "We have a student council meeting before class starts and have to be there early. Got to run. Love you, and see you on Saturday afternoon."

"I'll call tonight."

"I've got basketball," he reminded her, sounding distracted, and she knew he was headed out the door with his cell phone stuck between his shoulder and his ear. His book bag no doubt hung off his free shoulder and his blond hair would still be damp around the edges. Many a time she'd seen him similarly head out of the house while on the phone with one girl or another.

Oh, yeah, she was reminded daily just how charismatic Daniel Travis had been.

"Call me after the game," she told him. "Love you. Bye."

"Love you. Bye," Ryan repeated their special farewell.

The phone line went dead and the instant connection to her son faded, leaving her lost and panicky at the tremendous events that would occur before the day ended.

She clutched her phone tightly in her palm. A week away from Ryan felt like forever. They'd never been apart more than two nights. Yet she couldn't have brought him with her as she'd done on previous business trips.

No way would she risk him and Daniel seeing each other.

Sure, she'd dreamed of them meeting for fifteen years, but reality wasn't dreams.

Reality was being a single mom so the man you'd given your heart to could have his dreams.

Sighing, she pushed away from the window, checked her sleep-deprived appearance in the mirror one last time, and left the hotel room.

Time to go face her past so she could move on with her future.

* * *

Dr. Daniel Travis glanced at his Boston Memorial Hospital schedule and sighed at the thought of yet another marketing person shadowing his every move.

He shouldn't complain. Thousands of lives around the country and eventually around the world would be improved because of the specialized three-lead pacemaker for congestive heart failure patients.

But even better, Cardico had agreed to fund his next research project once the pacemaker had been successfully launched. A project that, if triumphant, would fulfill his dreams.

From the time his dad had died from complications of heart surgery, Daniel had wanted to be a cardiologist. Specifically he'd wanted to come up with a better way to perform a coronary artery bypass graft, or CABG. A Staphylococcus infection had set into his father's leg after the donor vein had been removed and the infection had spread throughout his weakened body.

Daniel knew there had to be better ways than grafting one's own veins, which required a second surgical site. Cow and pig valves had been used for years for heart valve replacements. Why couldn't animal veins be used as donor grafts? Daniel believed they could, and he planned to test that theory.

He would find a way to keep people from dying so needlessly.

Not once had he ever strayed from his goal of preventing what had happened to his father from occurring again.

Daniel scrubbed up, then he entered the cardiac lab. Once there, he slipped on his sterile gloves.

He shivered at the frigid temperature, but from experience he knew the heat from the lights and the knowledge he held someone's life in his hands would soon have him sweating. Although a fairly simple procedure, he never took life for granted or how quickly the tides could turn when you placed a foreign object into someone's heart.

Each person he worked on was someone's husband, wife, sister, brother, mother, father, loved one. If he messed up, more than just the patient paid the consequences. That alone made him take his time, do the best he could each and every time he became directly responsible for someone's life.

From the corner of his eye he noted the audience at the far side of the operating room. With their light blue scrubs, face masks, hair bonnets, and shoe covers, the group of seven were medical students and the Cardico marketing executive.

He preferred to meet the sales representatives prior to them observing, but this one hadn't arrived until late last night and he'd missed the scheduled meeting with her that morning. One of his research study patients had been rushed into the emergency room due to fluid overload. He'd stabilized her and the ongoing study was not compromised. Besides, he didn't feel guilty at standing up Kimberly Brookes as her rescheduling had already held up his schedule two times too many.

Out of courtesy, more than anything, Daniel said a quick hello to the woman having the pacemaker placement. Sedation flowed into her via the IV in her right wrist and although she was awake, she wasn't lucid. He always made face-to-face contact with his patients prior to a procedure, visually and mentally making sure he had the right person.

Ellen Mills, sixty-seven, obese, and suffering from severe fatigue, shortness of breath, dizziness, and bradycardia, a slow heart rate caused by a left bundle branch block.

Daniel glanced at the monitor, mentally reviewed his pre-op notes, then watched the operating room nurse clean the woman's chest with antiseptic. Next, she placed an adhesive drape around the area where he would make the incision.

With Ellen readied, he picked up a sterile blade and made a two-inch straight cut a couple of inches beneath her left collarbone, slicing through skin and tissue. Using an imaging device called fluoroscopy to guide his movements, he painstakingly inserted the pacemaker leads into a large vein, easing the wire to the heart.

Daniel funneled a lead to the desired area within the right atrium of Ellen's heart and screwed it into the muscle wall, making sure it was securely anchored. Next, he inserted a lead into the right ventricle and screwed it into the heart wall.

The last lead always proved the most difficult and riskiest of the lead placements. With single-minded focus and steady hands, he threaded the third lead through the coronary sinus and into the left ventricle, checked placement, then screwed the lead into the thickened heart tissue.

The operating room nurse dabbed a hint of moisture from his brow.

Daniel carefully double-checked the wire placements and made sure all three leads remained in the desired spots. He slid the thin square battery-operated generator into the incision and anchored it to where he wanted it to rest for the eight or so years that the unit would reside inside Ellen.

Daniel smiled. It would be eight years before the unit needed to be replaced compared to the former six. Two extra years before a patient had to go through the procedure again, thanks to Cardico's advanced battery technology.

The computer chip in the generator would sense when Ellen's heart needed to beat and would pace the rhythm to make the heart eject blood efficiently.

First watching the monitor screen to ensure the pacemaker functioned properly, he stitched up the incision. When he'd tied off the last stitch, he removed his gloves and squeezed Ellen's hand.

"I'm finished, and everything went perfectly. I'll be by your hospital room later this afternoon to check on your progress," he told the woman.

Still a bit dazed, Ellen clasped his hand and nodded. "Thank you, Dr. Travis."

Daniel nodded, then turned to the students and the Cardico representative. He would give a guest lecture later in the week, but for now the students' instructor would review the procedure with them. However, Daniel's job entailed meeting and greeting Kimberly Brookes.

Despite wearing identical surgical garb to the students, he immediately spotted her. As the students removed their face masks, she stood slightly to the left of them. Even through the baggy blue fabric, her femininely curved body caused his gaze to linger in appreciation. Truth be told, his noticing surprised him as months had gone by since the opposite sex had held much interest for him.

Besides Ms. Brookes's delectable body, he could see her tension. Anxiety radiated from her every pore. Was she weak-stomached and the procedure had got to her? As placing the device involved very little blood, few got squeamish or light-headed. Very few.

Annoyed at what he suspected would cause yet another delay, his gaze lifted to hers.

He knew those eyes.

His body tightened with tension and his own stomach weakened.

What the hell was Kimberly *Duff* doing in his cardiac lab?

CHAPTER TWO

DANIEL pulled himself together with lightning speed, quickly masking his shock at seeing his one-and-only heartbreak.

His Kimberly had gone to nursing school and worked for a medical equipment company? Last he'd heard she planned to go to California to pursue an acting career after she finished high school. Perhaps Hollywood hadn't glittered quite as brightly as she'd thought.

A nurse.

She'd changed her mind about more than just him, it would seem.

His gaze dropped to her bare hands, which pressed flat against the wall behind her, as if for support.

Was she as shocked to see him as he was her?

She couldn't be. She'd known all along who she was coming to meet. Known, and delayed for as long as possible by rescheduling twice.

A slow grin spread across his face as the truth hit him.

She'd been worried about seeing him.

Which meant she still had feelings for him after all these years. Feelings strong enough that she feared them coming face-to-face.

Her eyes widened ever so slightly at his mirth, and she nervously moistened her lips.

Desire flickered through him. Hot, wet desire that shook the floors of Boston Memorial Hospital and threatened to knock Daniel off his feet.

Just the sight of her pressed to the wall turned him on, made him want to push against her, grind his body into hers, and hear her call out his name.

He took a step toward her, closing the distance between them, then stopped cold.

What was he doing?

Fifteen years had gone by. Brookes, not Duff. She was married. She'd dumped him for some guy she'd met while he'd been away at school.

He had no right to touch her, and even if he had, he was at work.

"Daniel." His name came out as little more than a hoarse pant from her pale pink lips.

Her discomfort did little to ease the wild plethora of emotions hitting him or his unwanted surge of libido. Years had gone by since he'd experienced such a reaction. Perhaps since the last time he'd seen her.

"Kimberly," he said with a sarcastic edge, taking in everything about the woman before him. The long lashes fringing her eyes, the fullness of her lips, the smooth texture of her creamy skin, the curves beneath her hospital-issue scrubs.

Her lashes lowered, she took a deep breath, and met his gaze with a dreadfully faked bravado. "I hear wonderful things about you, Dr. Travis."

No wonder she hadn't gone into the acting business if this was the best she could do.

"Funny." He leaned in, resting his hand on the wall a few inches above her shoulder, resisting the urge to touch her hair. Was it as soft as it looked? As he remembered? Lifting an eyebrow, he stared down at her taut expression. "I've heard nothing about your exciting acting career."

She flinched at his words. Her cheeks reddened, and she flashed a glance at a couple of lingering students who curiously watched them.

"No." She didn't meet his eyes. "I don't suppose you have."

Her quiet words sent thunderous aftershocks through him. Made him feel like a jerk and, quite probably, he was because he'd meant his words to sting.

Not that he'd expected them to. Ice coated Kimberly's heart, protecting her from anything he could throw at her.

At least, it had.

This wasn't the feisty, bubbly girl he'd known. She'd have come back spitting fire at him and leaving him whimpering from wounds.

What had happened after he'd left Georgia that Christmas break?

The guy she'd dumped him for hadn't been a Brookes.

She straightened from the wall, unintentionally putting their bodies in near contact, and met his gaze head-on.

What he saw in her soulful eyes almost sent him stumbling backward.

Hurt and betrayal shone in their green depths.

Why did she look hurt?

She'd been the one to throw away their relationship.

Seeming to realize she'd revealed too much, she pasted a smile onto her terse face and held out her hand.

"As you know, I'm Kimberly Brookes, with Cardico.

It's good to at last meet the great Dr. Daniel Travis." She spoke loudly enough for the students to hear her professional, aloof tone.

Daniel's gaze dropped to her outstretched hand. She expected him to pretend like he hadn't known her, *in the biblical sense known her,* all those years ago? Did she think no one would guess by the way he'd greeted her? By their body language?

He searched her face, but she'd pulled herself together and he saw only what she wanted him to see—nothing at all.

Longing to touch her and knowing they were being watched, he clasped her hand.

Her fingers warmed his skin, felt small within his grasp, yet held power over every nerve ending in his body. He would have lingered, investigated the phenomenon of her skin against his, but she jerked away with the urgency of someone being scalded.

He felt pretty burnt to a crisp himself.

Just as in the past, skin-to-skin contact between them ignited flames and left him dancing in a hazy smoke cloud, trying to catch his breath.

"Let's get out of here." Not waiting for an answer, he grabbed her elbow, ignored the smoldering lust, and guided her from the cardiac lab.

"Wait, Daniel," she protested, digging her heels in the moment the lab door closed behind them. "What are you doing?"

Hearing her say his name after so long made his stomach lurch.

"Giving us some privacy." Which standing in the middle of a hospital hallway didn't provide.

"Privacy?" Fear shone on her face. "We don't need privacy."

"You expect to spend the next week with me without us ever being alone?"

She blinked wide green eyes and nervously chewed on her lower lip. "I'm sure we can avoid being alone for the most part."

"Maybe if you'd come when originally scheduled and you'd have had the benefit of another marketing representative with you." He wanted her to know he had made the connection to the fact she'd put him off and he guessed her reasons. "But as you opted to come at a later date, it's just you and me."

She winced. "I was delayed."

He just bet she had been.

A tall brunette resident Daniel recognized shot him a smile and a flirty wave. "Hi, Dr. Travis. You were amazing, as always."

"Hey, Angel," he absently responded to the young future cardiologist while he tried to figure out what he wanted to say to Kimberly.

Kimberly's eyes rolled. "Some things never change, I see."

She made it sound as if he'd cheated on her. Wasn't that the pot calling the kettle black?

"What's that supposed to mean?"

The skin around her mouth paled. "Just you."

"Me? You haven't seen me for fifteen years, so don't judge me based on what you think you know."

His blast of fury surprised them both and earned several questioning glances.

Kimberly took a step back and looked around the

hallway, nervously letting her gaze settle on the closest exit sign. Did she plan to make a run for it?

Why would she run from him?

Then again, he had just jumped down her throat.

Two nurses watched them with unabashed curiosity. Daniel shot them a glare, and they busied themselves.

Raking his fingers through his hair, he took a deep breath. "Look, I'd rather not have this discussion in the hallway of the hospital where I work. As it is, we've given the gossipmongers fodder for the next month. I don't need any help in that department."

"Fine." Her expression resigned, Kimberly nodded. "Let's go somewhere private and get this over with."

Wordlessly, Kimberly followed Daniel, keeping her eyes focused anywhere other than on the tall man leading her down the path of forbidden thoughts.

She didn't know exactly how she'd expected him to greet her, but she hadn't anticipated the hunger in his eyes.

Or how just being in the same room with him would send her body into shock.

During the procedure, she'd literally leaned against the cold wall to keep from sliding to the floor. Her inability to hide her unprofessional reaction had earned her several snide looks from the medical students. No wonder. They'd probably assumed she'd been fighting nausea or dizziness.

For that matter, she *had* fought nausea and dizziness, but not because of witnessing the pacemaker placement.

If only they'd known the real reason her head had spun, her body had sagged, and her heart had raced.

What had she been thinking to come here?

She should have turned in her resignation rather than face Daniel.

Had she really thought coming face-to-face with Ryan's father wouldn't destroy the delicately-knit framework of her life?

No matter how much she'd told herself otherwise, seeing Daniel changed everything.

And why had she attacked his character with her snide comment? Even if Daniel had whisked *Angel* into his arms and passionately kissed the resident, *she* had no right to complain.

Yet she'd wanted to complain, loudly and with great gusto.

"This way," he said, pointing her to the left, where they went through a set of double doors.

She followed him into an area designated for hospital staff only, a back hallway that ran behind the specialty clinics, allowing the doctors easy access to the hospital without having to go through their patient waiting areas.

He punched in a security code on a computerized wall panel that caused an audible click.

They went through the unlocked double doorway, and he led her to an office marked with his name. Unlocking the door, he pushed it open, allowing her to enter first.

Unable to prevent her curiosity to do with everything about him, she made note of the steel and black décor.

A bold, black desk monopolized the room, drawing her attention first. Off to the side were an imposing black leather sofa and two chairs with a magazine-littered chrome-and-glass coffee table between them. She could picture Daniel consulting with a patient there.

Or stretched out, taking a quick nap on the sofa after wrapping up a late-night emergency.

A bookshelf lined one wall, full of textbooks, a few knickknacks, including several heart models, and a single photo frame. Without taking a closer look, she recognized the woman embracing Daniel.

Leona Travis.

Even across the room she could feel the woman's eyes boring into her, asking what she was doing, bothering Daniel after all this time. Didn't she know she still wasn't good enough for her beloved son?

Daniel's mother had nothing to worry about. Kimberly wasn't there to steal Daniel away from his precious career. Far from it.

She risked a sideways peek at him. He watched her with an odd expression on his face and she winced at the sheer force of pent-up longing that came with looking at him.

A multitude of emotions hit her. Guilt, panic, curiosity, need, lust.

Lust.

How could she feel lust for a man she hadn't seen in years? And not just lust like "I'd like to do it with you," but lust like "I'm going to rip off your clothes and have you, right here, right now."

Crazy lust that consumed rational thought.

Oh, she was in so much trouble.

She stared into blue eyes identical to her son's and shook her head, backing a few steps farther into Daniel's office. "I should leave."

"Don't be ridiculous." He stepped toward her, all predatory male with his female quarry in sight, making her feel small and claustrophobic.

Why did he look at her that way? Like he wanted to kiss her? She'd been prepared for indifference or anger or just about anything other than his sexual interest.

That she'd never dared let herself consider.

"Why would you leave?" he asked, his long, lean frame dominating the room and drawing her gaze to how his scrubs outlined his broad chest and narrow hips. "You just got here."

"I don't think I can do this." She fought to keep a businesslike façade, but knew under the circumstances it was a losing battle. In truth, she trembled on the inside and couldn't decide if from fear or desire.

"This?" A dark blond brow arched.

She put her hand to her temple, realized what a telltale motion she'd made and dropped shaking fingers to her side. "Work with you."

He shrugged, drawing emphasis to the muscles bunching beneath the short sleeves of his scrub top. "It's just a week."

Just a week? Ha. Look at what a mere hour had done.

Fifteen years' worth of telling herself she didn't need him, that she'd imagined how intensely he affected her, crumbled to leave her defenseless and exposed. How was she supposed to survive an entire week of forced proximity?

As it was, she'd likely spend the rest of her life trying to purge the image of Daniel, all testosterone-oozing grown man, from her mind. Trying to forget eighteen-year-old Daniel had been bad enough. The sexy specimen in front of her would require a full-blown case of amnesia.

"I'll contact Cardico," she thought out loud. "Tell them something has come up, that I've got to go home."

"Home being Atlanta?"

Absently, she nodded, then paused. She shouldn't tell him anything. What if he followed her? Found out about Ryan?

She was being silly. What reason would Daniel have to follow her?

Her blood hammered in her ears, making thinking difficult, but she assured herself she had no worries about Daniel following her. Not once in fifteen years had he shown any sign he regretted stepping out of her life. She may have been the one to end things, but he'd let her go without putting up a fight.

"Surely working with me for one week isn't that bad? None of the other Cardico employees have had complaints." He looked all too relaxed for him to have been the one surprised by their meeting. "You might recall that I'm quite adept at teaching you new things."

How dare he bring that up? Probably as he'd intended, memories of Daniel teaching her body how to please and be pleased flooded her mind.

"Just think of all the things I can teach in a week," he continued in a low, husky voice.

"I'm not a silly, easily seduced virgin anymore, Daniel. I'm a grown woman."

His eyes raked over her, making her acutely aware of her grown-woman body. "Exactly."

She took another step back and bumped into his desk.

Nowhere left to run.

She'd prepared for this, and yet he had her on the retreat. Had her brain foggy with need unlike any she'd ever known, not even for him.

He was calm, cool, and collected. Like seeing her was no big deal.

Life could be so unfair.

"The wise thing to do would be to have Cardico replace me with someone else," she reasoned, trying to keep her head above water but knowing she was drowning in the seductive depths of Daniel's eyes.

"The wise thing? Since when have you opted to do the wise thing?" His forehead wrinkled, and he leaned closer, so close she could smell him, all musky man with a spicy aftershave that revved her senses into hyperdrive like it had when he'd leaned toward her in the cardiac lab. He smelled divine. "You're a total daredevil."

Not anymore. Not since…him.

"Besides, why should you be replaced?" he continued. "Because we were once lovers? That's a ridiculous reason for Cardico to replace you, and you know it."

"I should have known better than to come here." A person had to know when to retreat. The time was now. Before she gave in to the desire to refresh her memory of how he felt, tasted. She craved a taste of those lips. His lips. Her gaze focused on the amused tilt of his mouth, the tilt that said he knew what she was thinking. "I did know better," she admitted.

"Why did you?" He trapped her in the intensity of his stare. "You knew you were coming to me, that we'd see each other, and be forced to spend time together. Time doesn't change some things, like physical attraction. You had to know what might happen. Yet you chose to come. Is that why you're here, Kimberly? Did you come alone, without your husband? To see what would happen between us after all this time?"

Her husband?

She jerked away, paced across the room, focused on

the photo of him and his mother on his desk, because the picture provided a dose of cold reality. "Nothing is going to happen, Daniel. Not between us. Not ever again. This is crazy."

"So what's new?" He didn't sound heartbroken at her revelation. "I've always been crazy when it comes to you. Why should now be any different?"

"Because any physical attraction between us ran its course a long time ago." A lie if she'd ever told one— she felt his pull as strongly as if he were a powerful magnet and she a cheap scrap of metal. "We're working together. You're supposed to train me on the CRT, not seduce me."

"Seduce you? Is that what I'm doing?" His voice held a teasing edge, and she hated it that he could find humor in the whole situation when she felt like a helpless mouse, with him playing the tomcat. Sure, she'd seen shock in his eyes in the cardiac lab when he'd first realized who she was, but then he'd relaxed like she was just another memory.

She probably was just another memory.

"I'm going home."

He laughed, a hearty sound that made her knees weaken and angered her to strengthen her resolve.

"Running away, Kimberly?"

"Yes," she admitted, before thinking better of it. Turning, she found he'd followed her across the room. Inches separated their bodies and she longed for the safety of being hundreds of miles apart.

"I've never known you to run from anything." He cupped her chin, lifting her face toward him, staring into her eyes. Confusion darkened his gaze. "You're scared of me?"

To death.

He could take away what she held most dear.

If she didn't get her act together right now, he'd see she was hiding something, and he wouldn't let up until he knew the whole sordid truth.

"Don't say things like you know me. You don't," she pointed out, much as he had earlier. Only she kept her voice calm, steady, despite his fingers burning into her flesh. "Why wouldn't I be afraid of you? You're making my working life hell."

His lips thinned to a tight line. "You've changed. The girl I knew never ran. She faced her fears, conquered them."

"Of course I've changed," she scoffed, wanting to pull free from his hold but knowing that would only reveal how strongly he affected her. "I was little more than a child when you knew me." Only a couple years older than Ryan was now. "I'm a grown woman and have grown-up responsibilities."

"Like to your job?"

"Yes, to Cardico and to…" She sealed her lips to stop Ryan's name from leaving her treacherous mouth. Unable to meet Daniel's gaze any longer, she twisted to free herself from his hold.

"Go on. To who? Your husband?"

"I'm divorced." She could have bitten her tongue for revealing that tidbit. The less Daniel knew about her personal life the better, and she didn't want to discuss her brief marriage with him. "I was referring to my mother."

If her marital status surprised him, he didn't let his shock show. "I thought she died last year."

"You heard that?" Her mother hadn't been a prominent citizen or anyone important other than to herself and Ryan. "How?"

"My mother still lives in Peachtree. She mentioned seeing the announcement in the local paper."

Kimberly nodded. How many times when visiting her mother had she been tempted to drive up Daniel's street? To travel down memory lane?

But she never had. She wouldn't risk running into Leona. Daniel's mother had a clear idea of what was good for her son. And what wasn't.

Kimberly and Ryan fell into the second category.

Besides, she'd have had to face the hurt in her own mother's eyes if she'd sought out Leona in any way.

"How is she?" she asked of the woman who'd played such an instrumental role in the direction her life had taken fifteen years ago.

His mouth twitched. "Getting older and wishing I'd move home."

All the blood drained from Kimberly's body and pooled in the pit of her stomach, causing it to churn with nausea, but she kept her expression bland, feigning little interest.

"You're thinking of moving back to Georgia?" Lord, she hoped not. "Why would you move to Georgia?" she mused out loud. "Your research is here in Boston. Heart patients worldwide need you."

"I can do my research anywhere," he snorted, dismissing her words when she'd expected him to puff up with egotism. Most of the men of her acquaintance would have done so when given such an ego stroke. "But I have no plans to return to Atlanta."

Outwardly pretending she couldn't care less, she bit back a sigh of relief.

"I think we should call a truce."

Surprised, she met his gaze. "A truce?"

"Short of you faking a major illness, in which case I suspect Cardico would either reschedule your training yet again or fire you, you're stuck here for the week."

He had a point. As much as she'd like to just walk away, she had a great job at Cardico. Ryan would be leaving for college in a few years. Tuition wouldn't come cheap. And, there were her benefits, like health insurance and so on. Unemployment, even if just for a few weeks, wouldn't be a smart risk.

"What kind of truce?"

"We'll behave on a professional level while at the hospital, treat each other with respect."

Sounded feasible. In theory.

"When we're not at the hospital?"

"Any time we spend together outside work…" he flashed a mouthful of perfectly straight teeth in a smile that had sin written all over it "…we'll decide how to deal with moment by moment."

"Fine," she agreed, vowing to make sure she didn't see him outside the hospital.

She'd do her job, give Cardico their money's worth, but beyond that she'd stay clear of Dr. Daniel Travis.

And maybe, just maybe, she'd survive this week.

CHAPTER THREE

"How long have you had increased difficulty breathing, Mrs. Johnson?" Daniel asked the woman sitting in a chair in one of his exam rooms.

He worked in a cardiac clinic within Boston Memorial Hospital that connected to his private office. Ten cardiologists in total practiced at the clinic. His patient schedule was lighter than normal today due to the time set aside for Cardico.

For Kimberly.

Although tiny crow's feet fanned her eyes and her body boasted maturity that hadn't been there the last time he'd seen her, time had only added to her beauty. She looked amazing.

Plus, she carried herself with a grace she hadn't possessed at seventeen.

Grace and confidence.

Because for the rest of the morning after they'd left his office, she'd been nothing but the smooth professional.

Even now she was in the cardiac lab, watching a CRT pacemaker placement performed by one of his partners, Dr. Gregory Jessup. Greg would be relocating to

Nashville in a few weeks to take a cardiology position with Vanderbilt Hospital and would head up implementing CRT placement in Tennessee.

He guessed Kimberly opted to go with Greg to avoid more time with him, but he'd given her the choice.

"Dr. Travis?"

Daniel blinked.

"Dr. Travis?" The older woman wrinkled her nose and swatted him with the magazine she used to fan herself.

"Sorry, Mrs. Johnson." He'd done it again, blanked out with thoughts of Kimberly. Never did anything come between him and his patients, but today he admitted he'd been distracted by a collision of his past with his present.

Pull yourself together, Daniel. You're dealing with people's lives.

He looked into Mrs. Johnson's dark eyes and gave her his full attention. "You were saying?"

The woman gave him an odd look, then returned to fanning the magazine back and forth. "I was saying that I've not been able to catch my breath for at least two weeks. If I walk from one end of my apartment to the other, I have to sit down and I feel wheezy. My apartment ain't much more than a speck on a breadcrumb so it ain't that much of a walk, yet I can barely do it."

Daniel made a few notes on the computerized notebook that contained Mrs. Johnson's electronic chart. "Have your feet been swelling more?"

"Lord, yes." She lifted a foot off the floor and waved it at him. "I can't even wear real shoes anymore because these elephant trunks won't fit in them before the day's done."

"What about your hands?"

She held up chubby fingers. "I haven't worn my wedding band in weeks because the last time I did I had to take an extra fluid pill and use a stick of margarine to get it off."

Daniel sat the computerized clipboard on the counter, then listened to the left and right sides of Mrs. Johnson's neck. Her carotid arteries both sounded clear. No bruits, a tiny swishing sound that blockages made. Then he listened to her heart. She had a grade-two murmur with mitral valve regurgitation caused by her congestive heart failure. Ronchi could be heard in both lung bases.

"Cough," he ordered her.

She did so. The wet rattle didn't clear.

"I'm going to order a chest X-ray and an echocardiogram. You might recall that an echocardiogram is an ultrasound of your heart and isn't painful." He leaned back, watching her reactions to his words so he could fully address her concerns. "Your heart isn't pumping blood efficiently enough and fluid is building up in your lungs. That's why you have the rattling sounds in your chest called ronchi, and it's why you feel so tired and out of breath all the time."

Her dark eyes bore into him. "Can you fix me?"

"I want to look at the test results first but, regardless of what they show, we're going to make some changes to your treatment program."

She nodded.

"We'll need to increase your fluid medications. You'll have to have blood tests more frequently to watch your sodium and potassium levels. As with your current medicine, the new pill can cause your potassium levels to drop. This is dangerous for a variety of reasons, but one of the major ones is that it can cause muscle spasm. Your heart is a muscle and the electrolyte imbalance can throw it dangerously out of rhythm."

Mrs. Johnson's eyes widened.

"As long as you get your blood tests when you're supposed to, we'll be able to keep your potassium level close to where it's supposed to be."

She nodded.

"I'm going to give you some literature on a special type of pacemaker for congestive heart failure. It's designed to correct your heart's ability to contract, which will improve your ejection fraction—that's the amount of blood the heart pumps out with each beat. With improved ejection fraction, it will improve your congestive heart failure."

Her mouth twisted in confusion. "What does that mean?"

"It means that if you qualify for the pacemaker you'll be able to walk from one end of your apartment to the other without getting so short of breath." One of life's little blessings one didn't appreciate until the ability disappeared and exertion of any kind became a trial. "I think you qualify, but I want to see your echocardiogram before making a final decision."

Nodding her approval, the woman flashed a smile at him. "Sign me up, Dr. Travis."

"First we have to run the tests and you have to read the literature. We'll meet back in a few days to go over the results and make a decision on the CRT pacemaker."

Her forehead creased. "What's CRT?"

"Cardiac resynchronization therapy. It's a fancy way

of saying that it will synchronize the electrical activity
of the heart, making it beat as a complete unit."

Mrs. Johnson gave him a blank look and he attempted to explain again in simpler terms, but she shook
her head.

"If you say it'll make me feel better, that's all I need
to know, Dr. Travis."

He smiled, wrote out the order for the tests, and
said goodbye to the woman he'd been seeing for several months.

"I'll have Trina—" his nurse "—schedule these. I'll
check you again in a few days."

If Mrs. Johnson's tests came back showing her to be
a candidate for the CRT pacemaker, he'd squeeze her in
toward the end of the week so Kimberly would get to
observe.

Kimberly. He'd put her from her mind for…he
glanced at his watch…five minutes. She'd still be in the
cardiac lab.

And he had more patients to see and needed to keep
his mind off her.

Kimberly was brought to Daniel's office after Dr.
Gregory Jessup had finished the CRT pacemaker placement in an eighty-year-old woman. He pulled up a
computer video feed of a procedure Daniel had done
early on in the study phase, explaining how the device
worked and differed from other pacemakers.

"I've got to run to a meeting," the dark-eyed and
dark-haired doctor in his early thirties said. Dr. Jessup
had a quick smile that reached his eyes. He'd flirted a
little, but in a no-pressure sort of way. She got the im-

pression from his easygoing comments that he was just a natural flirt and one of those people everyone liked.

"I'll be fine," she assured him, smiling sincerely. "Thanks, Dr. Jessup."

"It's Gregory." He nodded at the computer screen. "That should keep you entertained until Daniel finishes with his patients. If not, there's always solitaire."

He shot her a wink and reluctantly left Daniel's office.

She watched in fascination as Daniel threaded a wire lead into the right upper chamber of a heart. With hands steady enough to make a neurosurgeon envious, he screwed the lead into the atrium wall. Two more leads followed. One in the right ventricle, one in the left.

The man was a brilliant cardiologist. She didn't have to have five years of cardiology nursing experience to recognize his skill.

Not only was he good at healing hearts, but also at making each patient feel important, special.

He'd always made her feel special, too.

Right up till she'd found out they'd made a baby.

Then everything had changed.

"You looked bored."

Daniel spoke from beside her, causing her to jump. She'd been lost in thought and hadn't heard him enter his office, much less come to stand beside her.

She glanced up, leery of the twinkle in his eyes. She didn't begin to understand how his mind worked, but found his smile irresistible and felt her own lips curving.

Hastily, she glanced at the computer monitor. "The procedure is fascinating, as is the CRT pacemaker. I wish I understood all the aspects of how it works."

He laughed. "Don't worry. By the end of the week you'll be wishing I'd shut up about the CRT."

"I doubt that." She'd always found her job fascinating. Unable to stay away, her gaze returned to him. "I hope it's okay that Dr. Jessup let me wait here."

"No problem." He watched her a moment then his gaze lowered to her mouth.

Feeling edgy at his closeness and how he looked at her, she bit her lower lip.

"Tell me about the battery Cardico developed," she said to cover her nervousness. As long as she kept things businesslike between them, she'd be fine. *Right.* "I know it's supposed to last longer, but this is the first pacemaker to make use of it. Why did we opt to go with the CRT first?"

His gaze slowly lifted. His blue eyes pinning her, he shrugged. "It's a good fit, I suppose. The CRT is designed to give improved quality of life and the patient not having to go back into surgery for eight years rather than six is a definite improvement."

His words were all business, but the way he said them came out seductive. Or perhaps that was just her overactive imagination. Or the way his eyes said totally different things, like that he'd made note of her gnawing on her lower lip.

"The battery was originally tested at Boston Memorial Hospital?" Kimberly gulped.

"With an Ivy League college so close and the teaching environment of the hospital, doing research here comes naturally." He leaned near, clicked on the mouse, dragging the arrow to the box to turn off the video feed. His arm brushed her shoulder in the process and she bit back a squeak. Whether from his touch or the yummy way he smelled wasn't clear and didn't matter. Business conversations weren't supposed to be so…hot.

"I don't think," he continued, still close enough she could feel his body heat warming her, "I'd like practicing at a facility that didn't stay at the cutting edge of technology."

"No, I suppose not," she agreed, shooting a quick look at his thoughtful expression. "But trying new things, that's risky, too. If your research is wrong, people die."

"All good things come with risk. If one isn't willing to push the boundaries, to try new things, one has to accept the current state as the best one can ever be."

She could almost believe he spoke about more than medical research. Almost.

"I'm very proud of you, Daniel." The words came out soft, sincere but held the impact of fingernails scraped across a blackboard.

Or, better yet, a bucket of ice that quenched the flames flickering between them.

Because there was nothing warm about the way Daniel's eyes looked when he spoke.

"Your sentiments are meaningless to me."

CHAPTER FOUR

AFTER his continued good humor during the morning and his sexually-charged looks, Daniel's sharp words caught Kimberly off guard.

Had their truce gone up in smoke so quickly?

Gritting her teeth, she stared at the screen without seeing anything. She knew he didn't care, but to have him so bluntly cut her to the quick opened a gaping wound in her heart.

Tears blurred her vision, but she fought them, refusing to let them fall, to let him see how his words had hurt.

How dare he be all nice and then hit her when her defenses were down?

"Come on," he ordered in a gruff tone that left her uncertain if he was upset with her or with himself. "You have a lot to learn in a short amount of time."

Without looking at him, she nodded. "Fine. I'm ready."

Not really, but the sooner she learned all about the CRT, the sooner she could go home. To Ryan.

That had her gaze shooting to Daniel, almost as if she expected him to have heard her thoughts, to know she'd given birth to their beautiful son.

"What?" he asked, staring at her.

She shook her head and followed him out of his office to make his hospital rounds.

They stopped by the nurses' station and Daniel introduced her to a couple of nurses who seemed friendly enough, if slightly disinterested in her. However, their eyes ate Daniel up.

She had no right to be jealous, she reminded herself. No right.

She wasn't jealous.

She was hurt. Hurt he'd so easily dismissed her pride in him. Although silly, she felt a stake in his success. After all, she'd given up what might have been so he could live out his dream.

His easy camaraderie with the female hospital staff served to contrast starkly how stilted their enforced togetherness really was.

Fighting to keep a professional expression on her face, she shadowed Daniel, smiling at appropriate times, nodding when indicated, but inside she fought a hollowness that threatened to engulf her in darkness.

"How are you feeling, Ellen?" Daniel asked, entering a hospital room with Kimberly close behind him.

"Hungry," the woman admitted from her bed. She had a sling on her arm to prevent movement from working the pacemaker loose. She'd wear the sling for a couple of days to keep her arm immobile.

"That's a good sign." Daniel flashed a smile that caused Kimberly's heart to speed up.

So warm. So caring. A blessing to any patient who had the good fortune to have his services.

Seeing him, watching him work, assuaged any

thoughts of whether or not she'd done the right thing in ensuring he went to medical school, of taking that small role in his success. Daniel was living out his dream.

"This is Kimberly Brookes." He introduced her to his patient. "She works for the medical equipment company that makes the pacemaker I placed in your chest this morning."

Mrs. Mills's gaze shot to her and Kimberly gave a friendly smile.

"She observed your procedure," Daniel continued, crossing to stand next to the woman's bed. He shook a short, overweight man's hand, presumably that of Mr. Mills, then studied the heart monitor screen hooked up to Ellen. When satisfied, he put on his stethoscope and listened to her heart and lungs. "Everything sounds perfect," he told his patient, then looked up at Kimberly. "Want to listen?"

Was he granting a peace offering or just doing his job? Regardless, she nodded. She took his stethoscope, trembled at the thought that she now held an extension of who Daniel was and placed the tips in her ears.

"May I?" she asked the patient, just to make sure Mrs. Mills didn't mind.

The woman nodded. "The more who listen, the better chance nothing will be missed."

Daniel gave a hearty laugh. "Good point, but I assure you that your heart is working better than it has in years."

Kimberly placed the diaphragm against the woman's chest, listening at all five of the crucial points. Steady rhythm, steady rate, with only an extra click giving notice that the pacemaker was there.

"Wonderful." She smiled. "Thank you for letting me listen."

"You're welcome," Daniel and Mrs. Mills answered simultaneously.

Daniel winked at his patient. "Great minds and all that."

He quickly checked Mrs. Mills's ankles and feet. Minimal swelling, Kimberly noted, but the woman had ulceration on her little toe that should be seen about by her family practitioner.

"Mrs. Mills, I'm going to ask for a podiatry consult for your feet," Daniel said, closely checking between the woman's toes.

Even better. Kimberly smiled again. Thorough to the end, even when the problem wasn't directly related to what he was treating.

"I don't like the look of the sore on your left little toe and you have some macerated skin between your toes on both feet."

"They don't bother me much. Just get sore occasionally." The woman dismissed his concerns.

"Still…" he flashed another smile "…can't have me fixing your heart and your feet slowing you down."

Kimberly saw three other cardiac patients with him and accompanied him during a pre-op consultation for CRT placement with a sixty-nine-year-old barrel-chested woman named Sarah Allen, who'd opted to schedule the procedure for the following morning.

"Go over with me why I'm getting a pacemaker again," the woman said, batting her lashes at Daniel in a blatantly flirtatious way.

Kimberly almost smiled.

"Basically," Daniel explained, taking her wrinkled

hand in his, "the electrical signal that tells your heart to contract is hitting the right side of your heart the way it should. But, in your case, it moves to the left side too slowly. This causes the four heart chambers to contract out of sync. When the out-of-rhythm chambers contract, blood isn't pumped efficiently through your body. This leaves your body hungry for oxygen."

"And this pacemaker will make my heart chambers work together again?"

He nodded. "The CRT conducts an almost simultaneous electrical impulse to all four chambers, generating proper in-sync contraction, and will have you feeling like a new woman almost immediately."

Daniel explained more about what the woman should expect from the procedure. "Kimberly will be in the cardiac lab tomorrow when you get the CRT pacemaker."

Kimberly smiled at the curious woman. "I work for the company that makes the pacemaker. Dr. Travis is training me this week." The woman didn't seem impressed, actually seemed annoyed at Kimberly's inclusion in the conversation. So Kimberly started over. "That's a gorgeous Afghan rug on your bed. An amazing piece of craftwork." She'd noticed the brightly colored design the instant she'd entered the room. "Did you make it?"

Old blue eyes shifted to Kimberly, looking at her properly for the first time. Visibly, her demeanor changed.

"My granddaughter did." The woman smiled, tenderness shining in her bright eyes. "She brought the Afghan for me to wrap up in tomorrow after the procedure. When I had my gallbladder taken out, I nearly froze afterward." Arthritic fingers clutched the knitted rug. "She said I'm not going to be cold tomorrow."

"No, I'd say not." Kimberly shook her head, running her fingers over the beautiful pattern. "Your granddaughter did an excellent job. You must be very proud."

"Taught her myself."

Having put the woman at ease, Kimberly chatted with her about her procedure while Daniel made notes in the chart. She would make notes herself on why the woman had opted to go with the CRT. Had it been because of Daniel's recommendation or had there been second-opinion consults? She asked other questions that might come up when she started marketing the pacemaker.

The more she learned, the better she could do her job.

Of course, if she told the truth, she'd admit she found working with Daniel fascinating.

There had never been a time when she hadn't found everything about Daniel Travis fascinating.

Which explained why she found this week so scary.

Late that evening, Kimberly sat in an upscale Boston restaurant eating delicious seafood fresh from the Boston harbor. If she hadn't been so nervous, she'd have said the company was quite nice. Two of Daniel's partners had joined them, along with two local Cardico employees, one female, one male.

Walking into the restaurant they'd caught the eyes of several people. With Daniel looking fabulous, Dr. Jessup holding his own in any crowd, and the local Cardico employees having that svelte one-of-the-beautiful-people professional salesperson look, no wonder people stared with interest.

Honestly, she and Tom Underhill, a slightly balding cardiologist, probably stuck out like sore thumbs. She'd found herself sitting between Gregory and Tom, which had left Daniel sitting across from her, sandwiched between her Cardico colleagues. The female Cardico employee obviously had a thing for Daniel, but otherwise Kimberly instantly liked the busty brunette.

Candlelight flickered on each table, giving the restaurant an intimate air. A basket of melt-in-your-mouth dinner rolls tempted her to have another. Just one more, she thought, biting into one and thinking she'd crash later from so many carbohydrates—but the mouthwatering taste was worth it.

"I just love your accent," Tom said to Kimberly, sucking the meat from his crab leg. "I think we should just all shut up and listen to you talk."

"You never say that about my accent," Daniel reminded his partner from across the table, the slight furrow between his brows the only indication he might be serious.

"Yeah, well, there's a reason for that." Gregory smiled good-naturedly. "Shut up, pal."

"I'm just saying that I'm from the South, too." Daniel's tone sounded laid-back, amused, and she got that cat-and-mouse vibe again. "Just outside Atlanta, as a matter of fact."

Kimberly shot him a warning glare. She'd prefer the table not know they'd once known each other.

"That's where you're from, right?" Sage asked, taking a sip from her white wine. She looked back and forth between Daniel and Kimberly and must have seen something. "Did you two know each other?"

"Atlanta is a big city." Kimberly forced a smile and took a calming drink of her soda. She'd forgone alcohol as she didn't want to risk letting her guard down around Daniel. "Fortunately."

Having driven to the restaurant, Daniel opted for soda as well, but Kimberly noted the others enjoyed various alcoholic beverages. Perhaps a bit too much, based on the noise level of their laughter.

"Oh," Gregory teased, while Tom ribbed Daniel, too. "I think you just got put in your place, bud."

"Good thing my ego isn't easily bruised." Daniel smirked. His gaze lazily challenged Kimberly.

They'd gone back to a semi-peaceful truce after his brusque comeback to her praise of his accomplishments, but she trusted him about as far as she could throw him. Not even that much. She wouldn't let her guard down, wouldn't open herself to his scathing remarks again.

Staying away from him, keeping distance between them while not at the hospital, was her number-one priority and if she could have gotten out of this dinner, she would have. Room service and her laptop suited her needs just fine.

But tonight was business, of sorts, and had been arranged by her Cardico colleagues prior to her arrival.

Fluffing her dark hair, Sage giggled. "I'm sure any number of women would volunteer to stroke your ego, if needed, Daniel. Myself included."

"Now, Sage, hon, you know it would never work between us." Daniel's blue eyes skimmed the marketing representative, then landed back on Kimberly. "I've always had a thing for blondes."

"I could go blond for you," the slightly tipsy brunette flirted.

Kimberly desperately pretended the conversation

meant nothing to her, that she didn't even hear the exchange. Because listening to a beautiful woman hit on Daniel was not her idea of a good time.

Actually, the thought of coming to Boston and meeting the woman in his life had tortured her ever since she'd found out she'd be spending a week under Daniel's tutelage.

But there didn't seem to be a permanent woman in his life. Just a multitude of wannabes.

"You're beautiful just the way you are." Daniel smiled, causing a dimple to dig into his left cheek.

Kimberly wanted to crawl under the table. Why did he have to be so sexy? If he'd lost all his hair and had a paunch, she might have survived this week without the beginnings of an ulcer.

"And I'm sure Robert prefers you as a brunette," Daniel continued.

Just hearing his voice reminded Kimberly that Daniel's attraction went much deeper than his looks. He had a magnetism that would shine through even if he lost all his hair, teeth, and gained a spare tire. Daniel's appeal came from within and just happened to be deliciously eye candy–coated as an added bonus. Who was Robert?

"You're right," Sage agreed with a frown. "But it could have been fun giving it a whirl, and I'm so mad at Robert that I'd like to give his neck a whirl." She sighed softly. "You could at least be a gentleman and make him think there's a reason to be jealous."

Daniel laughed, and that was the end of the exchange.

Or so a relieved Kimberly thought.

Gregory poked her with his elbow. "Just for the

record, that's not Daniel's usual mode of operation when it comes to the opposite sex."

"Oh?" she asked, feigning little interest.

"Robert and Sage are having problems, but they'll work them out." He shot Sage a questioning look and she nodded with a slight huff. "Daniel doesn't make moves on other men's women. Actually, he doesn't have to make moves at all, because the women chase him. I hadn't been on the cardiology unit but a few days before the legend of Dr. Daniel Travis made itself known."

"It's the nurses' and interns' fault," Tom said from Kimberly's right. "They love to pretend Boston Memorial Hospital is their very own real-life soap opera."

Daniel grimaced, but didn't say anything.

"Daniel plays the role of Dr. McDreamy, with all the women walking around wanting to run their fingers through his hair and stare into those baby blues," Gregory said, grinning mischievously toward Daniel. "I've been thinking about getting contacts."

"No piece of plastic is going to hide the nonsense in those brown eyes," Daniel warned with a glare from the baby blues in question.

Kimberly took a sip of her soda and wished she'd ordered something stronger. She really didn't want to hear this.

How the heck had they even started on the subject of Daniel's prowess with women?

One minute they had been having a friendly discussion, the next one of her colleagues had been hitting on Daniel, and the next his partners were telling her about his sexual prowess.

Like she needed a play-by-play.

Not.

"Me and the rest of the boys live vicariously through him," Tom continued, ignoring Daniel's wry comment. "Women fall at his feet as if he really was one of those television doctors. A through and through bad boy when it comes to the ladies, that's our Dr. Travis."

Gregory lifted his glass in a salute to Daniel's expertise.

Kimberly scowled. "Gee, maybe he should have gone into gynecology. That way he'd have a ready supply of women with their legs spread."

"You weren't paying attention," Daniel scolded, looking amused. She suspected it was her flustered expression entertaining him, though, rather than his partners' admiration.

"Getting women to spread their legs isn't a problem," he clarified, giving her a knowing look that stripped her bare and had her knees defensively clenched together beneath the table. "Never has been."

Kimberly's mouth fell open. How dare he? Anger shot through her at the telling gleam in his eyes.

"If you're implying—" Fortunately the singsong buzz of her cell phone cut off the tirade she'd been launching into. A tirade that would have revealed too much. Way too much. About the past. About the present and how he currently affected her. About how the television-doctor stuff burrowed under her skin and infested her with jealousy.

Flashing a look of disapproval at Daniel, she murmured, "Excuse me."

She answered her phone without looking to see who the caller was. "Hello."

"We won!" Ryan's voice came over the line, pulling her to reality with a quick thud.

"That's wonderful, dear," she answered, acutely aware that, despite the conversation going on around them, with his boys still extolling his studly virtues, Daniel's attention zeroed in on her phone call. Could he hear Ryan?

Murmuring another "Excuse me" to no one in particular, she got up from the table and headed to a back hallway that led to the restrooms. Not wanting to talk to Ryan in the ladies' restroom, she lingered in the empty hallway.

"I scored fourteen points and had eight assists. Tyler hit six foul shots in a roll, and Jonathan fouled out at the end of the fourth quarter." Ryan's words gushed, without pausing for a breath. Kimberly smiled at his excitement. His exuberance for life always energized her.

"I wish I could have been there." She smiled politely at a woman coming out of the restroom with two toddlers held protectively in her grasp. "Sounds like I missed a great game."

"Me, too, Mom. It was an awesome game. You'd have loved it." Someone spoke to Ryan and he answered, probably with his hand over the speaker as his words were mumbled. When he returned his attention to her, he said, "Tyler's mom's taking us out for pizza to celebrate. That okay?"

"Sounds like fun. Just make sure you aren't up too late and that you finish your homework."

"I always do," he said, and she could just picture him rolling his eyes.

"I know." She smiled, feeling lighter just from hearing his voice, feeling that special bond between them.

"Just didn't want you getting any ideas, with me being out of town, kiddo."

"Hmm, maybe I will take a night off," he teased.

"You'd better behave."

"Aw, Mom, you just won't let me have any fun. Don't you know that when parents go out of town, it's a kid's responsibility and civil duty to be wild and throw parties?"

"Kimberly?"

She glanced up and saw Daniel squeezing past a group of young girls who'd just come out of the ladies' room. Curiosity shone in his eyes. And concern.

Although he'd clearly been on his way to the men's room, he crossed his arms and took on a protective stance. "Everything okay?"

Dear Lord, how long had he been standing there?

Heat suffusing her face, she gave him a quick nod. "Fine."

"Fine? Are you sure, Mom?" Ryan asked, clearly not believing she'd agreed with his assessment. "I get to be wild and throw parties?"

Although she wanted to look away, her gaze held Daniel's. Just being so near him while on the phone with Ryan, looking into eyes identical to their son's, tightened her throat.

"Sorry, but, no," she clarified, "you cannot throw wild parties. I was speaking with—" *your father* "—the heart surgeon I'm training with this week."

"Cool." Ryan sounded duly impressed, but quickly became distracted when someone spoke to him. "Gotta go, Mom. We're headed for pizza."

Why didn't Daniel walk away? Do whatever it was he'd come to do?

Her heart thundered against her rib cage, but she'd perfected her professional persona years ago and knew she looked poised even if she felt anything but. "Have fun," she told their son.

"'Night, Mom. Love you. Bye."

"'Night, Ryan. Love you. Bye," she automatically repeated, aching with how much she missed him.

"Who's Ryan?"

Keeping her emotions masked, she clicked her phone shut and clasped the cellular device tightly in her palm.

"My son."

CHAPTER FIVE

"You have a son?" Daniel's head spun. He'd been on his way to the men's room when he'd overheard Kimberly's side of the conversation. A gentleman might have kept going or pretended he hadn't heard. Perhaps that's what he should have done.

Kimberly had a son.

She'd been married. Of course she'd have children. He should have realized. Still, the thought of her as a mother boggled his mind. Try as he may, he couldn't imagine her curvy little body swollen with child.

She glared at him with a stubborn set to her chin. "My personal life is really none of your business, Daniel."

"But you do have a son?"

"Do you not understand what 'none of your business' means? Just because we called a truce for work, it doesn't mean you have a right to anything about my personal life. Go." She glanced around the hallway with a touch of desperation he didn't understand. "Go make your boys proud and pick up some hot babe or something. Just leave me alone."

"No." He should leave her alone, but being confronted with the one woman from his past whom he never quite got over made "should" a moot point.

Her gaze lifted to him. "What do you mean—no?"

"Just that." He liked how, in anger, gold flecks dotted the green of her eyes, giving them a catlike appearance. "I'm not going to leave you alone. For the next week, you belong to me."

All day his emotions had flip-flopped between anger, lust, surprise at seeing her, and feelings he couldn't begin to label, but he knew his words to be true. He didn't want to leave her alone.

"That's ridiculous, Daniel," she huffed. "I work for Cardico, but they don't own me. No one does, and certainly not you." She straightened her shoulders and placed her hands on her hips.

"That's not what I meant, and you know it."

Her eyes darkened to a forest-green and she outright glared. "If you've been sleeping with your former trainees, I understand how you're getting such glowing reviews, but I'm off-limits." She pursed her lips. "Been there, done that, remember?"

Ignoring the last bits, he grinned. "Are you saying I was a good lover, Kimberly?"

He hadn't slept with any Cardico employee and, despite the way his pals told it, very few others. He liked women, liked sex, but hadn't taken the time to pursue either in months. Not since a ski trip to Colorado with his last girlfriend and they'd ended the moment she'd started hinting she'd wanted more. Relationships didn't seem worth the energy these days, and sex for the sake of sex had stopped appealing years ago.

Which begged the question of exactly what he wanted from Kimberly. Because he'd never trust her with his heart again, yet he definitely wanted sex. If it wasn't sex for the sake of sex, then what was it?

"No." Color rose up her neck.

"No, you're not admitting I was a good lover, or no, I wasn't? Because I distinctly recall you enjoying it when I touched you." To prove his point he grazed his knuckles across her cheeks. The caress was for her benefit, but his heart quivered at the contact, proving instead how much he'd enjoyed touching her and apparently still did. Just as he enjoyed teasing her, seeing the real emotions flutter across her face before she could hide beneath her professional veneer.

"Just no." She inhaled sharply, squeezed her eyes shut, and pushed at his chest. "Let me go, Daniel. Please, let me go."

Immediately, he backed away. She looked scared again, like she had in his office.

He didn't understand her fear. He'd never hurt her in any way. She'd dumped him, not the other way around. Even on the night they'd made love for the first time, he'd done everything he'd been able to to ease her passage into womanhood.

Memories spilled forth, making him long for the past when she'd claimed to love him. Not that her love had been more than a teenager's passing fancy, but he longed for her looks of hot desire all the same.

That's when reality hit him full force.

"I've tried, Kimberly," he admitted, all teasing gone from his voice. "For fifteen years, I've tried."

Perhaps the look of desperation that had come over

her face prompted him to admit the truth, to tell her things no sane man would admit to his ex-girlfriend.

"I want you." Saying the words out loud felt right. "As much as I did fifteen years ago. Possibly more. Oddly enough, it doesn't bother me that I want you."

Her hands stilled on his chest and she looked torn, tormented.

"What does bother me is how you look at me with fear in your eyes." Like she was doing right at this moment. "How you act like a frightened rabbit, with me playing the role of the big, bad wolf. Which makes me wonder who put that fear in you."

Her mouth opened, then closed. Her eyes did the same.

"None. Of. Your. Business." Each word came out with an emphatic burst of defensiveness, and he knew he'd hit on the truth.

His fists clenched against the wall in synchrony with the squeezing of his heart. He longed to smash in the man's face who'd hurt her, to give him a dose of his own medicine. Because someone had hurt her. Someone had changed her into a woman afraid of taking chances, probably her ex-husband.

He longed to see the carefree smile she'd so easily worn in the past. Instead, he saw a flurry of dark emotions tightening her lips.

"For the next week, everything about you is my business."

Her lips didn't curve into a smile. Not that he'd expected them to. Not yet. But he would make her smile, make her laugh, and in the process he'd get her out of his head forever, because this time it would be him who brought things to an end.

"You can't just decide something like that, Daniel." She shook her head in denial. "What was between us ended fifteen years ago."

"No, it didn't." It had smoldered like hot coals, just waiting for the right moment to burst into flames. And not just on his part. She could say what she liked, but he'd seen her looking at him throughout the day, caught the longing in her eyes. The moment was now, and fires raged between them that he refused to ignore. "You feel it, and so do I."

"Don't tell me what I feel," she insisted, warily eyeing a businessman on his way to the restroom, reminding him that they stood in a restaurant hallway.

"Fine," Daniel said after the man had passed. "I'll tell you what I feel. I want you."

"You've already said that."

"You didn't believe me."

"I believe you want to take me to bed." She sounded annoyed.

"And?"

"And that's a horrible idea, Daniel. My only reason for being here is to learn about the CRT, not to have a fling with you."

No, having a fling would mean taking a risk, and she didn't seem to do that anymore.

"It must be difficult, being a mother and trying to fit in dating, too," he commented, watching her face. "You do date, don't you, Kimberly?"

She scowled. "Of course I date."

"Really?" he asked lazily, lowering his lids to half-mast while he eyed her lush lips. Lips he longed to lean forward and kiss, but even more he wanted her to admit she wanted his kiss.

His eyes met hers.

She did want him.

She couldn't hide the fact that he affected her. That being near him made her aware of her own body.

He'd remind her how good it could be between a man and a woman because he suspected she'd forgotten.

"Tell me, Kimberly," he gently encouraged. "When's the last time you went on a date?"

She opened her mouth, no doubt to remind him what wasn't his business, but he covered her lips, slowly kissing her in a seductive tease.

He'd forgotten how sweet her mouth was, how her lips seared through him straight to his heart.

He didn't lean in, didn't press his body to her in case her fear returned, but he wanted her beneath him, their bodies tangled together.

Her mouth met his, allowing him access, an access he could barely resist. Only the thought of where they were, of their lack of privacy, kept him from plunging in and to hell with the consequences.

He pulled back a lock of hair, stared into her glazed eyes.

"Don't bother denying it or telling me it's none of my business, because we both know you want me, too, Kimberly. Just as we both know that I'll be spending the night in your bed before you go home. By fighting the attraction between us, you're only robbing us both of the pleasure I'd give you."

"You're insane," she breathed against his mouth, but without fear or pulling away. Only hot desire shone in her wide eyes.

He wasn't clear who moved, but their bodies touched from where her hands rested against his chest to where his groin pressed into her belly.

"Certifiable," he agreed. Getting involved with Kimberly after she'd done such a number on him all those years ago was foolish. Yet he had a week with her. A week to give her back her smiles, which any fool— specifically him—could see she needed. A week to work her out of his system once and for all.

It was a win-win situation.

Daniel didn't turn down odds like those.

"Oh, there you two are," Sage said, her eyes flickering back and forth between them, a knowing look on her flushed face.

"Were we lost?" Daniel didn't move away from Kimberly, just kept her pressed between the wall and his hard body.

He'd have held her close, kept his hand in the small of her back while guiding her to the table so anyone could see she belonged to him. But by frowning and giving a curt shake of her head, she made her feelings clear. She didn't want anyone to know what happened between them.

She twisted away and, without another look at him or Sage, headed into the ladies' room with her shoulders held high and rigid.

She may want him every bit as much as he wanted her, but she wasn't ready to admit to her feelings.

Then again, he'd never quite believed she hadn't still wanted him when she'd dumped him for another guy.

Oh, God. Daniel had kissed her.

Oh, what a kiss.

Hot, heavy, sweet, the kind of kiss that made a girl forget she stood in the back hallway of an upscale Boston restaurant.

Kimberly had.

She'd totally forgotten they were dining with a group of colleagues, forgotten they stood in a public restaurant, forgotten they were little more than strangers with a past.

And a son.

She sighed, staring at her reflection in the mirror.

Her makeup was smudged and her lipstick completely rubbed off her kiss-swollen lips. Onto Daniel? She hoped not as that might raise questions with the others.

Her eyes shone brightly, looking large and luminous in her pale face. She pinched her cheeks, hoping to add some color to her skin. Too bad she'd left her purse at the dinner table because she could really use a powder touch-up and lipstick.

The door opened, and Sage entered.

"Hi," Kimberly said automatically, then winced when her voice squeaked. She was a thirty-two-year-old professional, not a silly schoolgirl. Why was she acting like she got caught with her pants down in the boy's locker room?

But Sage didn't comment. Walking up to stand next to Kimberly, she checked her appearance and took a factory-sealed lipstick from her sling purse.

"Here," she said, handing Kimberly the tube. "This came in one of those freebie gifts I always get when I purchase my wrinkle cream. You need a fresh coat and this is more your color than mine anyway."

Her face red, Kimberly took the warm coral-colored cylinder, removed the clear plastic, then applied the creamy substance to her lips.

"Thank you," she said, attempting to hand the container back to her work colleague.

"Keep it. As I said, the color looks better on you than it would on me." The woman fixed a stray strand of hair, then leaned against the counter and eyed Kimberly. "You're one of Daniel's exes?"

One of Daniel's exes?

She tried not to wince when she realized that described her to a T.

Sure, he'd been much more in her heart, but he'd walked away without looking back.

Well, apparently he'd not forgotten her body. Just look at how quickly he'd moved from her walking back into his life to wanting to take her to bed. Typical man, she supposed, but it hurt to think she'd meant so little.

"He's watched you all evening, you know?"

She had caught him looking at her several times. Not that he'd looked away when their eyes had met. He'd just given a lazy grin and kept right on staring. Like he wanted her to know he wanted her and he intended to have her.

He'd kissed her in the hallway and she hadn't wanted him to quit. Not ever.

She'd longed to lean on him and let him hold her, tell her that she'd made the right decisions, and he understood. But as she had no intention of telling him a thing, those desires didn't make sense.

"He was a year ahead of me in high school," Kimberly admitted. Denying Sage's curiosity wouldn't gain anything. The other woman already knew. Admitting the truth somehow made Kimberly less self-conscious that a business colleague had caught her sandwiched between Daniel and the wall. Less like just another skirt to be chased. "We went out a few times."

More than a few times, but she didn't have to tell Sage that her junior year had been devoted to spending every moment possible with Daniel. And they'd been nearly inseparable the summer before she'd started her senior year. The summer before Daniel had left for college in August.

August. The month they'd created Ryan, probably while lying on a blanket near Turkey Run Creek, staring up at the stars and desperate for every together moment they'd been able to squeeze in before they'd be apart for months on end.

He'd come home at Christmas, excited, exhausted, and eager to pick up where they'd left off. Only she'd faced responsibilities no seventeen-year-old should face in the months he'd been away. She'd done what had needed to be done. She'd let Daniel go. Set him free. He'd left, never to return. At least, not to her. The day she'd broken up with him had been the last time she'd seen him. Until today.

"For the record, I've never slept with Daniel," Sage clarified, interrupting Kimberly's thoughts. "We've been friends for several years. Despite my flirting with him, he's right about Robert."

What was she supposed to say? Kimberly wondered. That she was glad Sage hadn't slept with Daniel? She was. The thought of him with another woman hurt. Much better not to have faces to put with the pain.

"I've heard about Daniel's bedroom skills, though." Sage smiled slyly. "They say he's amazing."

"They?" Kimberly couldn't stop from asking. What

had happened to not wanting faces? The less she knew, the better.

"Daniel briefly dated a couple of my girlfriends. One for a few weeks. The other was just a weekend fling on a group holiday to the Caribbean." Sage took out a compact, powdered her nose, and nonchalantly added, "It was several years back, but they'd still both give their right eye to have Daniel look at them the way he looks at you."

Kimberly gulped, trying to clear the thickness clogging her throat. "How does he look at me?"

"Like he wants to take you home and gobble you up." Sage checked her appearance, then offered Kimberly the compact. "Take my advice—let him."

Let him?

She didn't sleep around. No matter what her past with him, no matter that they shared a son, no matter that she wanted nothing more than to make love with Daniel, they had no future together. Sleeping with him would be wrong.

Wouldn't it?

Because it wouldn't be love.

It would be nothing more than sex.

Awesome, out-of-this-world sex because it was Daniel, but still just sex.

Speaking of sex, after that hot kiss, how was she going to face him and pretend he didn't matter?

That she didn't want him every bit as much as he'd said he wanted her?

CHAPTER SIX

DANIEL slid into his chair and ignored Greg's curious look.

He didn't have to explain his actions to his friend. Honestly, he couldn't explain them to himself, much less someone else. He just knew that he wanted Kimberly. Enough that he could set the past aside and enjoy their week together.

One week to get their fill of each other.

His pager buzzed at his side. He lifted it from his waistband, glanced at the number, and sighed.

The hospital.

He called, spoke with the emergency room nurse, and hung up as Sage and Kimberly reappeared from hiding in the ladies' room.

Sage gave him a look that answered his question of whether or not she'd cornered Kimberly in the restroom. She had, and Kimberly had apparently satisfied her curiosity. Or at least up to a certain degree as he got the impression Kimberly was a private person these days.

No doubt he'd be cornered by Sage at some point in the near future, but not tonight.

"Come on, we've got an emergency," he told Kimberly, standing up, causing her eyes to widen with disbelief.

If he stood close enough to whisper in her ear he'd tell her that it wasn't that kind of emergency, but he liked how she thought. But she'd sat down across the table and clutched her fork in a way that made him think she'd jab him if he made a sudden movement. He settled for a quick wink that let her know he knew where her mind was and that he liked her thoughts.

"A patient has been admitted through the emergency room and I'm on call. He's in fluid overload and needs a workup for the CRT. I'm going to talk with the patient and his family and will likely schedule the procedure for the morning." Daniel gave her an innocent look. "Tonight's perfect timing for you to get extra training."

"Okay." Still eyeing him suspiciously, Kimberly nodded. She scooped her purse off the table and said something to Sage.

"Too bad I'm not on call tonight," Greg teased, still eyeing Daniel with an odd look. "Of course, I could go for you and you could stay and have dessert."

"I don't think so." Daniel shot his buddy a warning glance.

Greg laughed out loud, which irked Daniel. Sometimes his friend saw too much.

"Sage," Daniel said. "You okay with dropping Greg off at the hospital so he can pick up his car? Otherwise, the walk might do him good."

Sage batted her eyelashes at Greg. "I can do that."

"I'll see to it Kimberly gets back to her hotel."

"No problem," Sage assured him, giving Kimberly a conspiratorial wink. Kimberly's face flushed bright red.

The two had done some female bonding in the ladies' room.

Curious as to what had caused the crimson to stain Kimberly's cheeks, Daniel intended to question her later. Right now he just wanted to get her away from their audience before she became even more resistant to his affection.

He turned to her. "Let's go."

Kimberly stood at the foot of the hospital bed where the patient who had been admitted through the emergency room lay. She reminded herself to stay focused on the task at hand and not on the doctor examining the peaked-looking man.

Daniel hadn't bothered changing into scrubs and still wore the khaki slacks and white shirt he'd had on at the restaurant. He studied the man's electronic chart and Kimberly studied him while pretending her interest stemmed from professional curiosity.

He'd already reviewed the emergency room doctor's notations and was now taking note of the vital statistics the nurse had recorded after he'd been transferred to his room.

Evert Reed had been battling congestive heart failure for several years, but had recently started having acute fluid overload which his high-dosed diuretics had failed to prevent.

"Dr. Kelley has you on intravenous furosemide to take the fluid off your lungs," Daniel explained to the elderly man, who was propped up on two pillows and visibly struggling to breathe despite oxygen being delivered by a nasal cannula.

Two women in their late forties vigilantly observed from chairs along the hospital room wall. Both were the patient's daughters and introduced themselves as Virginia and Estelle.

Daniel acknowledged them with a nod.

"Your wife?" he asked the man, his voice soft and full of compassion.

Kimberly admired how he looked at the whole picture and was trying to get a feel for the man's support system as that greatly impacted recovery.

"Our mother died last year," the older of the two women said when her father looked helplessly at her. Talking required too much energy, and he didn't have the strength. Perhaps he had trouble talking about his deceased wife.

"Dad lives by himself now," the younger daughter added, giving her father a concerned glance.

"After he's released from the hospital he won't be able to stay alone for about a week," Daniel advised, looking directly at the women. "When he goes home, I'd recommend an alarm system that he wears around his neck just in case he has problems."

"He can stay with either of us," the older offered. "My daughter just left for college. He could stay in her room."

The younger woman nodded her agreement.

"After the pacemaker placement, he's not to do any pulling or tugging. He'll possibly be able to go home the day after tomorrow if the procedure goes as expected."

"That soon?" the women asked, looking back and forth at each other. Panic registered in their eyes.

"It's what we'll plan on, but of course it all depends on how he does during surgery and how he responds afterward, but I don't foresee any problems."

The women gave each other a frightened look. "That seems so quick. We don't know CPR or anything like that. Are you sure we should take him home that soon? That we can take care of him?"

Daniel shook his head. "Nothing's for sure at this point, but if it makes you uncomfortable, not knowing CPR, there's a class offered through the hospital. Basic first aid and resuscitation is good for everyone to know. You should stop at the front desk and sign up for the next class."

Both women nodded.

"I would feel better if I knew what to do if Daddy couldn't breathe."

"Me, too," the other agreed, her gaze going to Kimberly. "Are you a doctor, too?"

"No." Kimberly shook her head. "I worked as a cardiac nurse in Georgia for five years, but currently I'm employed by the medical company that supplies the pacemaker Daniel, uh, Dr. Travis will be placing in your father's chest."

"Really?" The woman looked fascinated. "I guess I never thought about where doctors got stuff like that."

Kimberly smiled. "Most people don't."

"I…need…a…drink," the patient said between pants, calling their attention back to him. Both of his daughters immediately jumped to their feet to do their father's bidding.

"I'm sorry, but you can't have anything by mouth tonight. I can get one of the nurses to swab your mouth to moisten it, but that's it."

Daniel handed Kimberly the electronic chart and she glanced over it, skimming Evert's medications as that's what Daniel had pulled up and must want her to review.

Immediately, she spotted a problem. "Daniel?"

"Hmm?" He didn't glance up from checking the man's feet and ankles.

"Did you notice anything on his medication list?"

The hint of a smile told her he had noticed and was testing her. Either the attending physician in the emergency department or the medical transcriptionist putting orders into the computer had mistakenly left Evert on his high-dose oral medications for fluid, despite the fact that he was now receiving them by IV. Evert would have been double-dosed when the morning nurse gave him his by-mouth meds.

If he got any oral medication in the morning, which was unlikely as Daniel planned to write a nothing-by-mouth order until after Evert's pacemaker placement.

Daniel finished checking Evert and answered some of the family's questions. When they stepped out into the hallway, he grinned.

"Good catch on the medication list. I'll stop the oral meds when I write the nothing-by-mouth order, but I want whoever entered the order to be notified so the mistake won't happen again."

Kimberly nodded. Had the error not been caught and the nurse given the medication, Evert's electrolyte imbalance would have worsened. It could have thrown him into muscle cramps, organ shutdown, or even a heart attack.

She followed Daniel to a small dictation room and watched as he entered changes into the computer. He meticulously went over the record and put in orders of his own to prepare the patient for the planned procedure next morning.

He also spoke with the nurse in charge of Evert's

care, making sure she was aware of his plan to take the patient into the cardiac lab for pacemaker placement and the medication error.

- The computer would have sent a message to the pharmacy to cancel the oral doses, but Daniel liked to be thorough. Kimberly appreciated that. Too many times she'd seen assumptions made that had led to mistakes being made.

She watched his every action, admiring him more and more for his dedication to his patients, for the way he gave his all to what he did.

Although she'd worked with several excellent cardiologists, none of them compared to Daniel.

He really was the great Dr. Daniel Travis, heart surgeon *extraordinaire,* that she'd been hearing about weeks before arriving in Boston.

The great Daniel Travis she'd fallen in love with at first sight when she'd been only sixteen years old.

Based on the way his kiss made her feel, a lot of unresolved emotions still dwelled in her heart.

But, then, she'd never denied that she had strong feelings for Daniel. Hadn't that been why she'd done the things she'd done? Because she cared?

It was after ten by the time they left the hospital.

Kimberly sat in the creamy leather passenger seat of Daniel's sporty black Mercedes.

Although tired, her nerves jumped like a live wire.

Being alone with him on the way to her hotel triggered anxiety she hadn't felt when they'd rushed to the hospital to check on Evert Reed.

Would Daniel come to her room and attempt to seduce her?

Not that she'd let him.

She wouldn't.

But a girl needed a plan when thwarting the efforts of a man she desperately wanted.

She wanted Daniel.

Desperately. Insanely. Completely.

If she wasn't careful she'd be the one doing the seducing, and then where would she be?

Right where she wanted to be.

In Daniel's arms.

She gulped and stared out her window.

The drive from the hospital to her hotel only took a few minutes, but Kimberly's eyes drooped. At first to shut out the silence looming between them, but she hadn't slept the night before for worry at seeing Daniel, and exhaustion had caught up with her. She rested her eyes until Daniel pulled the car under the hotel awning. In only a couple more minutes she would have been fast asleep.

She expected him to hand his keys over to the valet, to insist he would accompany her inside, to at least steal another kiss, but he shook his head at the car attendant.

"I'm not staying."

"You're not?" She turned to him, failing to hide her surprise.

By the pleased look in his eyes she'd also failed to hide her disappointment. Disappointment she shouldn't feel since she didn't want him to stay. Not really.

Becoming involved with Daniel again would only complicate her life in ways she didn't need.

"It's late. We both have to be at the hospital early in the morning." He placed his thumb over her lower lip and gave it a soft tweak. "No worries, love. When we share a bed again, I won't have you so tired you're dozing off."

Her body shouted its protests as she climbed out of the car, smiled at the valet, and went to stand inside the hotel lobby.

She watched Daniel drive away, her heart crying that she was a fool for not persuading him to stay. What would one week of passion with Daniel hurt?

Besides everything?

Long into the night she pondered how with just a kiss he'd had her body aching for his touch. How with just seeing him so many old wounds had opened and threatened to spill all she held inside. Clearly, a good indication she needed to keep things just business between them.

Allowing Daniel to get close to her in any capacity was only begging for heartbreak, and how would she explain that to Ryan?

On Tuesday morning Kimberly arrived at the hospital bright and early to observe Evert Reed's CRT placement. The procedure went beautifully, with Daniel allowing her to stand directly beside him during the placement.

She spent the entire day with him, shadowing his every move and becoming more and more impressed with how he handled his patients and the attentiveness he gave to every detail of their care.

Fortunately, he stuck with his truce promise while at the hospital and never made an untoward gesture. He never even acknowledged the kiss they'd shared, and other than the times she'd find herself looking at his lips, she didn't either.

She actually enjoyed lunch, laughing as he recited

some of his more humorous patient anecdotes, with Gregory occasionally throwing in a punch line or two. But her nervousness about Daniel's plans for the night grew exponentially with each passing minute.

Would he offer to give her a ride to the hotel? Perhaps come inside for drinks? For her?

And if he did, what would she do? Because she'd be lying to herself if she thought she'd find the strength to say no.

But Tuesday night saw Daniel working late on a project that had nothing to do with CRT so she wasn't needed, and Gregory dropped her at her hotel.

She ended up ordering room service and eating in her hotel room. Alone.

As crazy as it was, as she needed to avoid Daniel at all costs, she missed him.

Insane. She really was insane.

She slept restlessly again that night. Dreams of Daniel seeing Ryan and taking her son away from her haunted her sleep. By morning, she wanted nothing more than to pack her bags and head home before she did something really stupid.

But she couldn't go home.

Wednesday went much as Tuesday. She spent the morning with Daniel in the cardiac lab, had lunch with him in the hospital cafeteria, and spent the afternoon observing him teaching a cardiology class on pacemakers to a group of medical students. She particularly enjoyed her visit to the university campus and found herself imagining how Daniel must have enjoyed living there during his university days.

That evening Kimberly did rounds with him to discharge a couple of the patients to whom he'd given pace-makers.

Kimberly wondered if tonight would be the night Daniel pushed to come to her hotel room.

She'd say no, of course, having decided that she couldn't handle a physical relationship with Daniel. But if he asked, she'd suggest going to dinner. Maybe they could talk—she could learn about his life now and if he was happy.

Right or wrong, sitting alone in her hotel room just didn't appeal when she could be with Daniel.

She glanced at him, thinking how handsome he looked in his blue scrubs, how they brought out the intensity of his eyes. How hard he worked and how admired he was within his field by the nurses, doctors, and the ancillary staff in the hospital. With good reason, his patients adored him.

"Hello, Mr. Reed. How are you feeling?" Daniel asked when they entered his hospital room.

"He's feeling much better," Estelle said from where she sat beside her father's bed. "His breathing is fine, even after the respiratory therapist took off his nose thingy."

"I can…talk for myself," Evert corrected his daughter, giving her an annoyed look. He turned his head to Daniel and flashed a toothless smile. "Hello, Dr. Travis."

Daniel walked over to the bed and returned his patient's smile. "I looked over your chart and your daughter's right—you are doing much better. Your oxygen saturations have been in the nineties this evening. I'm very pleased with how you're doing."

"We are, too," Virginia spoke up, dropping her knitting into her lap. "He's actually been laughing at things on television."

Kimberly smiled. The simplest things often meant the most and when you didn't have the energy to talk you sure didn't do much laughing.

Daniel glanced at the television. "*Gunsmoke*. What's Marshal Dillon up to tonight?"

A pleased smile on his face, Evert told all about the cowboy sheriff and his humorous sidekick while Daniel checked pulses in all four extremities and checked his feet and ankles for edema.

"Shh, Daddy," Estelle said when Daniel slipped on his stethoscope and listened to the man's chest.

When he had finished, Daniel handed Kimberly the stethoscope so she could listen. A regular heart rate and rhythm. No extra lung sounds, indicating that the fluid in Evert's lungs was resolving.

"Excellent." Kimberly nodded her approval. The adjective pretty much described everything Daniel touched.

Everything he was.

Time hadn't changed the parts of him that she found so entrancing.

Oh, how she hated admitting how much he got under her skin, but the more time she spent with him the more difficult it became to deny how he made her body feel. To deny what he did to her heart rhythm without the aid of a three-lead battery-operated device.

"You had an odd look on your face a moment ago," Daniel said after they stepped out of Mr. Reed's room. "What were you thinking?"

"Just that you're an excellent doctor, Daniel." She

wouldn't humiliate herself again by telling him how proud she was of what he'd accomplished.

As proud as if she'd been by his side the whole way and had crossed that graduation platform with him. Proud that Ryan's father was such a good man, such a good doctor.

Daniel stared at her long moments that made her wonder if she had something on her face or if perhaps he could read her mind, then he flashed a smile that melted her heart.

"Thank you." He turned, heading toward the next patient room scheduled for a visit. "I've got quite a bit of paperwork to go through after I finish making rounds, but how about grabbing a late dinner?"

Happiness flittered through her, making her feel lighter than she had in ages. *She should avoid him. She really, really should.*

But he hadn't said, *Let me take you back to your hotel room and strip you naked.* He'd offered dinner.

"I'd like that."

"Me, too." He grinned and went in to check on another patient, with Kimberly floating behind him.

Dinner with Daniel.

They'd have a chance to talk, catch up away from the hospital, and he wasn't on call tonight.

Excitement fluttered through her. Crazy excitement that her mind berated her heart for feeling.

At the end of the week, her heart would break.

She'd gone through the pain of losing Daniel from her life once. Did she really think herself strong enough to face that pain anew?

Yet wouldn't it be much worse to not spend every

moment she could with a man she'd given her heart to fifteen years ago and had never got back?

She hadn't. No matter what she'd told herself over the years, her heart belonged to Daniel. Always had, likely always would.

But minutes before they were preparing to leave the hospital an off-duty police officer took a bullet in the chest and all plans came to a halt.

The cardiologist on call was the injured man's cousin and he specially requested Daniel to perform the tedious task of removing the bullet from the left heart wall and trying to repair the damage.

Although the task before him offered little hope of success, Daniel, being Daniel, didn't refuse his colleague's appeal.

"I'm sorry," he apologized, pausing only long enough to tell Kimberly he'd see her in the morning.

"Me, too, but I understand." She bit back her disappointment, feeling ashamed that she dared feel loss when a man's life teetered in the balance.

"Kimberly?" Daniel's fingers tipped her chin, making her look at him. "Something changed this afternoon, didn't it? In Evert Reed's room? When you look at me now…"

She met his eyes, and could have lost herself in how blue they were.

"We'll talk later." He took a deep breath and gave a self-derisory shake. "I've got to get into surgery, stat. Wish me luck."

It wasn't what he was going to say. They both knew it, but Daniel had already headed to join the surgical team trying to save the police officer's life.

"Good luck, Daniel," she said, watching him disappear through a set of double doors without a backward glance.

Kimberly lingered in the hallway, feeling silly and out of place, but she hated to leave until she heard the officer's status.

Daniel would be in surgery for hours.

That was, if things went well, because the only way Daniel would finish sooner was if the officer died. Unfortunately, no one expected the man to make it through the surgery, much less through the night.

If the worst happened, she'd like to be there for Daniel.

She grabbed dinner in the hospital cafeteria and chatted with Gregory for a few minutes when he joined her at her table.

"You and Daniel knew each other in Atlanta?" he asked, eyeing her from across the table.

If she refused to talk, it would only raise Gregory's suspicions.

"We both lived in a small suburb outside Atlanta." She decided to tell Daniel's colleague the same thing she'd told Sage. "Daniel was a grade ahead of me in high school."

"Was he Mr. Perfect back then, too?"

"Mr. Perfect?" She hadn't caught any sarcasm in Gregory's tone, but she asked for clarification just in case.

"You know, popular, athletic, smart, good with the ladies?"

She laughed. "Yes, Daniel was all of those things."

So was his son.

"You and he were an item?"

How did she answer that? She wouldn't lie to one of Daniel's partners, but she really didn't want to discuss their past with a virtual stranger.

Then again, from watching them together, she could tell Gregory and Daniel were good friends and had been for some time.

"We were dating when he moved to Boston for medical school."

"He dumped you for Boston?" Gregory looked a bit incredulous.

"Not exactly." She wouldn't tell him she'd been the one to end things. For some reason, what Daniel's friends thought of him mattered, and she didn't want to sully his image in any way. "It was more of a mutual decision."

For a moment she thought Gregory was going to push for more details, but he took a sip of his soda. "And now work sends you here to him." He shook his head in wry humor. "Funny how life works, isn't it?"

Funny, indeed.

After a couple of hours of not hearing anything, Kimberly caught a cab back to her hotel and called Ryan. She caught her son and his friend playing their guitars. They sang a new song they'd written the night before and she listened over the line, her eyes closed, wondering what Ryan would say if he knew who she'd spent her day with.

When she arrived at the hospital early on Thursday morning, Daniel's nurse Trina told her that she'd find Daniel in the intensive care unit.

Aaron Clark, the police officer, had been admitted to the ICU and was in critical but stable condition. He'd miraculously survived Daniel removing the bullet and attempting to repair the heart wall.

Waving to the nurses, Kimberly stood in the ICU hallway, watching Daniel talk to the police officer's wife and teenage son in the open waiting area.

Although his hair was a darker blond than Ryan's, the teenager's height and built was similar. Seeing him brought home just how much she missed Ryan, how quickly he was growing up, and how soon she'd be all alone in life.

It also opened up another can of worms she didn't want to deal with.

Daniel was talking compassionately with the young man in a scenario that could easily have been a father talking with his son.

His hand rested on the boy's shoulder and he spoke to him with a directness that not many doctors afforded a teenager. The boy, struggling to be strong, nodded his head at whatever Daniel had said.

Daniel gave a reassuring squeeze and answered something the boy's mother had asked. His hand stayed on the boy's shoulder, allowing the proud young man to draw comfort from him.

Guilt belted her in the gut at the sight of what she'd denied Ryan all these years.

A father to guide him, offer support, and love him.

Guilt at what she'd denied Daniel.

A son who was his image. A son who would make any father proud. A son who was a wonderful young man.

She'd denied Daniel Ryan's childhood.

But if she'd told him, admitted to him that they'd accidentally made a baby, he'd have done exactly what his mother had warned.

He'd have stayed in Georgia, got a job at a local factory, and the world would have been cheated of a magnificent cardiologist.

Daniel would have forever carried his guilt over his father's death.

Perhaps he'd have resented Kimberly and Ryan for depriving him of his dream.

She shouldn't feel guilty.

She should feel proud, like she'd given him a wonderful gift.

But was there any gift, any career she'd trade for the last fourteen years of knowing and loving her son?

Her throat tightened and her eyes stung.

What had she done?

Her reasons had been valid at the time, her heart in the right place, but what reason did she have for not telling Daniel about Ryan now?

She realized what she had to do and fear stabbed deep into her heart.

A sound escaped from her throat, nausea threatened to gag her, and her hand flew to her mouth.

"Kimberly?" Daniel looked up from where he half sat on a chair's armrest. He flashed a tired smile. "You're early."

She quickly attempted to pull herself together. The last thing the Clarks needed was for her to fall apart in front of them.

She turned her gaze to Daniel and was struck by how haggard he looked.

Had he been here all night?

From the faint smudges under his eyes and the scruffy shadow on his strong jaw, she suspected so.

Her heart squeezed. Oh, Daniel.

She crossed over to where he sat with the police officer's puffy-eyed wife and forlorn son.

They made a sad-looking lot and her heart broke for them. Her heart broke for Daniel, too, for what he'd missed out on with Ryan. She resisted the urge to wrap her arms around them all and to have a good cry.

Then again, maybe she was the one who needed the hug and to cry.

Keep it together, Kimberly.

"I'm so sorry to hear about your husband and father," she offered. "Daniel's the best heart surgeon there is, so he's in good hands."

"Yes, that's what Aaron's cousin told me last night. That no one could do a better job than Dr. Travis." The exhausted-looking woman nodded, sending Daniel a grateful look.

The boy didn't speak, just fought the tremble of his lower lip and stared straight ahead, tears shining in his eyes.

That could be Ryan.

How would her son feel if something happened to Daniel and he'd never had the opportunity to know his father?

All these years Ryan could have had Daniel's love and support, and she'd denied it to him. Why?

The boy leaned over, said something in private to Daniel, and he nodded.

"Peyton needs a moment with his father," Daniel told them, oblivious to the heart-shattering pain ripping through Kimberly at every mistake she'd ever made.

Monumental mistakes that could never be undone.

Then again, with the way Daniel's eyes kept searching her face, maybe he wasn't so oblivious.

"It's not visiting hours," Daniel admitted. ICU stringently controlled visits due to the critical nature of the patients on the unit, but doctors could get away with bending the rules when the occasion called for it. "But I'm going to take him over and give him a minute."

Without a word to his mother, Peyton went with Daniel to ICU room number three.

The boy walked so rigidly Kimberly half expected him to snap. Poor boy, seeing his father like this had to be so difficult.

The mother in her cried for his pain and wished she could ease his suffering.

Through the glass wall Kimberly and Cathy Clark watched while Daniel and the boy talked next to his father's hospital bed.

Daniel's hand remained on Peyton's shoulder and from time to time the boy nodded at something Daniel said.

Probably Daniel was explaining the purpose of the tubes and machinery in hopes it would make the image of his father hooked to all the technology keeping him alive a bit less scary.

"He's really good with kids," Cathy commented, possibly to fill the silence or to distract herself from the harsh reality of the situation.

Kimberly cringed at the woman's word choice.

"Yes, he is," she mumbled, reminding herself that she had to keep it together until she and Daniel finished for the day. Then she could pour out her heart to him and, in the process, probably make Daniel hate her.

He would hate her. How could he not when he'd missed out on knowing Ryan?

Wouldn't she hate someone who'd stolen that from her?

Cathy's red-rimmed eyes met Kimberly's and the woman attempted a small smile.

"Does he have children of his own?"

CHAPTER SEVEN

REELING didn't begin to cover Kimberly's reaction to Cathy's question.

She opened her mouth to try to form a reply, but nothing came out.

The room spun. Her face flushed. Her heart slammed against her rib cage so hard it felt as if it bruised her insides.

She turned to Peyton's mother, but the woman seemed oblivious to everything but where her son stood next to his father's bed.

Did Daniel have children? Such an innocent question and yet one that held the power to set off a domino effect that would leave a lot of pain in its wake.

Kimberly's vision blurred and, fearing she might hyperventilate, she forced her breathing to stay steady, controlled.

How did she answer the woman's question?

Her heart wouldn't let her lie. She wouldn't say that Daniel didn't have children.

Yet there was no way on earth she was going to admit to a total stranger that Daniel had a son.

Not until she'd broken the news to Daniel first.

"Kimberly?" Daniel's voice cut through her dizziness. "You okay?"

She blinked up at the man standing beside her. Was she imagining him? Imagining the worried look on his face? The tenderness in his eyes?

Or was it just the fatigue making him look so concerned?

"I'm fine," she lied, knowing now wasn't the time or place to go into all the reasons she wasn't fine at all.

She shot a quick glance toward room number three.

Life didn't always provide a right time or place.

Sometimes a person had to say what was in their heart because they might not be given another opportunity. Ever.

"Peyton wanted a minute alone with his father." Daniel explained why he'd returned so quickly and why the boy remained in his father's room unsupervised. "He had some things he wanted to say in private."

"Oh, God." Cathy's face crumpled and tears rolled down her cheeks. "If Aaron doesn't…" Her voice broke and a sob shook her body. She leaned forward, her face in her hands, shaking with emotion. She rocked back and forth, sobbing.

Nurse mode and fellow mom kicking in, Kimberly wrapped her arms around the woman, hoping to offer comfort and perhaps needing a bit of her own and an excuse to escape Daniel's troubled stare.

"Shh, he's made it through surgery and the night. That's a good sign." From her years of working on the cardiac unit, she knew that was true. Those first few hours were the most critical.

"You don't understand," the woman cried, holding on

to Kimberly like a lifeline. "They argued yesterday evening. Peyton wanted to go somewhere and Aaron wouldn't let him." Several deep shudders shook the woman.

Kimberly hugged her tighter, offering soft comforting words.

"Peyton snuck out of the apartment—" Cathy sniffled "—and went anyway."

"Kids push boundaries," Daniel reminded from behind them, causing Kimberly to glance at him, then wince at the pain squeezing her heart.

She should have given him a choice, let him decide what he wanted from the moment she'd discovered her pregnancy. Instead, she'd lost him forever when she could have spent her life with him.

"It's a natural part of growing up."

The woman's eyes closed. She took several deep breaths and pulled back from Kimberly to give Daniel an imploring look for him to understand what she was about to say.

"Aaron went after Peyton. There were drugs being moved at the abandoned building where Peyton was meeting his new 'friend.' It was a setup to lure Aaron in. He was shot outside the building he'd followed Peyton to by a drug dealer he'd busted a couple of weeks ago."

She shot a weepy-eyed glance at where her son leaned over her husband's hospital bed. Tubes and wires poked out of his body at various points and Aaron's skin shone ghastly pale. The boy held his father's hand and even from across the hallway his pain penetrated them all.

"He blames himself for this." The woman wept. "If Aaron dies…I don't know what Peyton will do. I know it's not his fault, but he's so frustrated by life at this point

anyway, which is how this creep got to him so easily.
And now this."

Cathy curled into a crying heap.

Kimberly held the woman while she cried. A tear slid
down her cheek for the woman's pain. For the pain she'd
cause Daniel when she told him the truth.

For the pain Ryan would feel when she told him about
Daniel, that he could have had a father all these years.

"I think Peyton will be coming out in the next minute
or so," Daniel warned, his compassionate gaze going
back and forth between the weeping women.

Cathy sat up, wiping at her eyes and trying to control
her sobs. "I've got to be strong. He can't see me like this."

"It's okay for him to know you're hurting," Daniel
soothed. "Actually, he might be more confused if he
doesn't see you upset."

"Oh, he's seen me upset plenty," the woman admitted. "I've cried all night."

"Don't try to hide your emotions away from him. Let
Peyton comfort you." Kimberly gave a comforting squeeze
and felt such compassion for the woman she was com-
pelled to open her heart. "I have a son near Peyton's age."

She could feel Daniel's gaze on her as if blue velvet
brushed against her skin.

"He sees right through me," she continued, her
insides shaking, "when I try to hide things from him."
Except for the biggest deception of all, and she'd started
that one before he'd made his first appearance into the
world. "I've found that being honest with him about my
emotions and what's going on is the best route." Except
she hadn't been honest with Ryan. Not about his father.
"In many ways, he's my best friend."

How was he going to feel when he found out she had kept him away from Daniel all these years?

"Your son must be a very special young man." Cathy hiccuped.

"He is," she admitted. No child Daniel made could be otherwise. "So is Peyton. Make sure that through all this he knows that. You need each other right now."

She needed Ryan, to hug him and tell him how much she loved him. How sorry she was for her mistakes.

Cathy nodded.

When Peyton sat back down in the waiting room, the boy had a stern look on his face. He didn't speak, just stared into space. Daniel placed his hand on his shoulder, they exchanged a look of understanding, and Peyton mumbled, "Thanks."

"Kimberly and I need to make rounds on my other patients," Daniel said. "Then I'm due in the cardiac lab. I'll be back later to check on Aaron. If there's any change, the nurse will page me, but if you need anything, ask the nurses to call Trina at my office. She'll know where to find me."

Cathy nodded. Peyton gave a curt bob of his head in acknowledgment, but still didn't speak. He fought to keep his emotions inside, but they spilled forth like a tense veil.

Part of Kimberly hated to leave them, but Daniel was right. The boy needed time alone with his mother. Peyton wouldn't allow himself the luxury of crying in front of strangers. Hopefully he and his mother would be able to offer each other comfort and come out of this stronger.

She could only hope for the same between her and Ryan.

The moment they were away from the waiting area, Kimberly turned pleading, mascara-smudged eyes to Daniel. He almost winced at the raw emotions in her gaze and even before she spoke he knew what she was going to ask.

"Is he going to make it?"

"You're a nurse," Daniel reminded her. "You know as well as I do that there's no way for me to answer that question." He sighed, ran his fingers through his hair, and knew his current frustration came from a night of no sleep. "I never thought he'd make it through the surgery, much less the night."

"I'm sorry," she apologized. "I shouldn't have asked. It's just..." She stopped, her face pale except for the black marks beneath her eyes.

"Just what?" he gently prodded, wondering what was with her that morning. Had he pushed her too far when he'd pointed out what he'd seen in her eyes the night before?

He'd seen lust.

And more.

He'd seen longing and that bond they'd shared so long ago. A bond time had failed to break.

The bond that said they belonged together.

For the week, at any rate. He wouldn't think beyond that.

"Peyton makes me think of Ryan so much," she whispered in a hoarse voice. "I hate to see him hurting."

Ryan. It was so easy to forget she had a child.

Most of his heart patients were older, so he rarely dealt with children of any age, but he liked the ones he did deal with. Peyton Clark was no exception. He reminded Kimberly of her son?

"I'd like to hear more about Ryan someday." His comment surprised him. He hadn't meant to say anything about Kimberly's son, but it was true. Everything about her intrigued him, including the child she'd given birth to. Still, the thought of her bearing another man's child stung in ways he had no business feeling.

"You'd like him." A wobbly smile played on her lips and he'd swear she was about to start crying again.

The way she'd cried with Cathy had caught him off guard.

Had Kimberly given so much of herself to her other patients?

Caring so much was physically exhausting because there wasn't a way to save everyone. Unfortunately. Was that why she'd gone into marketing rather than continue in direct patient care? Because she hadn't been able to deal with the losses?

Some days he had trouble dealing with them himself.

"Perhaps we could go to dinner tonight? As we couldn't go last night?"

Daniel blinked.

They'd definitely reached a turning point the night before in Evert Reed's room. Something had changed and perhaps that something was acceptance of the way they reacted to each other.

Fighting it sure hadn't helped.

"I'd like that," he admitted, although he'd be exhausted. After pulling an all-nighter in the OR with only an hour's worth of rest on his office sofa that morning before starting back, he'd be ready to crash.

But a few more hours of being awake wouldn't hurt

when it meant getting to be with Kimberly. He could sleep next week after she left.

She smiled at him, a weary sadness in her eyes that he didn't understand, but her smile was real and for him and it stole his breath.

Made him question everything about the moment because it wasn't enough.

"Are you sure this is what you want, Kimberly? Spending time together that isn't business related?"

Slowly, she nodded. "I'm sure."

He almost believed her.

"Come on." Now wasn't the time for talking about the past, the present, or the future—not that he thought they had a future, but for this week he wanted to spend every free moment with her. "We have a full morning. Let's get started."

Daniel looked so exhausted by the end of the day that Kimberly was tempted to cancel their dinner date. But she needed to talk with him. She needed to tell him about Ryan. For that conversation they needed privacy, away from the hospital.

"Any place in particular you want to go?" Daniel asked when they were settled in his car. He drove to the exit of the parking garage and waited for her instructions before pulling out.

"Back to my hotel."

He spun toward her.

"To eat," she clarified. "You're exhausted, and it's been a long day. Let's just dine at one of the hotel restaurants so you don't have to drive so far to get home."

Not that she knew where home was for Daniel. She

knew nothing about his life now, so how could she feel
so strongly toward him?

Nothing about this man and her reaction to him
made sense.

He shrugged. "Okay."

He drove the car out of the garage and in the direction of her hotel. Heavy traffic clogged the streets, but
Daniel turned onto a back street and bypassed the
worst of it.

"Mr. Reed looked excited at the prospect of going
home," she said to fill the silence.

"Too bad his daughters didn't look as excited."

"They're scared of being alone with him."

"Taking care of an ill parent is a lot of work."

Something about his tone made her wonder if he
knew she'd cared for her mother those last few years.
But how could he? He hadn't even known she had a son
and being a mother was who she was all about. If he'd
ever checked on her he'd have known about Ryan.

He hadn't.

"The nurse went over discharge care and a home-
health nurse will visit him in the morning. He'll do fine."

She nodded and they began discussing another patient.
Eventually the conversation led to the Clark family.

"Dr. Bourne couldn't sing your praises enough on
how you handled Aaron Clark."

"He's not out of the woods yet." Daniel sounded tired.

"No, but just the fact he's holding his own is a
miracle. A miracle you gave that family."

"I'm no miracle-giver."

She smiled softly. "I'd argue that. I've seen how you
interact with your patients. Each time you're in contact

with them is a blessing. It's on their faces, in what they say to you, in how they respond."

"That's just doing my job, Kimberly. Not working miracles. My guess is you did the same when you worked as a floor nurse."

She'd like to think she'd made a difference in her patients' lives, in their families' lives, but did one ever really know what impact they'd had on another?

"You're very good at what you do," she praised.

"I'm one of the lucky few. I've always known I wanted to be a heart surgeon. I got to grow up and do the job I wanted. Not many people get to do that."

"No," she agreed. They didn't. If she hadn't had Ryan, what would she have done after high school? She'd told Daniel she wanted to go into acting and a serious relationship would hinder that pursuit. Pretending her heart wasn't shattering had embodied all the acting she'd ever done. She'd once thought of going into forensics, but that had just been the silly ponderings of a young girl who hadn't had a clue about life and the real world.

She'd chosen nursing because of the flexible work hours and the decent pay. A single mother had to consider those things when making career decisions.

Fortunately, she loved her profession.

"I worked hard, but I was also lucky that life gave me the opportunity to go after my dreams," Daniel continued, his hands loosely gripping the steering wheel.

Should she tell him now what she'd sacrificed for his dream? What he'd unknowingly sacrificed?

She stared at him. Although he watched the traffic and drove carefully, he looked relaxed. More relaxed than she'd seen him look since she'd met him again.

She couldn't bring herself to mention Ryan. Not yet.

Was it wrong that she wanted more time with him like this, before changing the world he knew?

She'd wait until later tonight, after they'd eaten, then she'd tell him.

Throughout dinner, they laughed, talked about Cardico, reminisced over old times, talking about things Kimberly had forgotten, times she grieved about for the sole reason that Daniel had loved her then.

Daniel drank a single glass of wine and, although Kimberly rarely drank, she had one, too.

"Why haven't you married, Daniel?"

"Never met anyone I thought I could spend the rest of my life with."

"But you might someday marry and have children?"

He shrugged. "Maybe, if I met the right person. But I don't feel any need to marry just for the sake of not being alone, and the world will go on even if I never have kids."

For a brief moment telling him he already had a kid played on the tip of her tongue, but she made a general remark instead.

When the waiter took their emptied plates, Daniel leaned back in his chair and smiled. "This has been nice, Kimberly."

"Yes," she agreed. "Very nice. We should do it again sometime."

His blue eyes caught hers and twinkled with mischief.

"Talk, that is," she clarified, giving him a scolding look that might have carried more weight if she hadn't been smiling.

"You free tomorrow night?"

Tomorrow night? Would he want to see her after she told him about Ryan tonight?

She had to hope for the best.

"Once this hard-working heart surgeon finishes with me, I'm free."

"And if he doesn't finish with you?" He picked up his wineglass and finished off the contents, but his eyes never left hers.

What was he saying?

Her heart thudded in her chest, so she couldn't catch her breath.

"Then I'm his and wouldn't be able to make other plans."

"My guess…" he leaned forward "…is that this heart surgeon is a pretty intelligent guy."

"Brilliant," Kimberly agreed.

"If he's that smart, he's not going to let you go that easily."

Oh, he'd let her go quite easily fifteen years ago, but she just smiled because thinking about the past would ruin the beauty of the moment.

"Which means you shouldn't make other plans for tomorrow night."

"Are you on call?" She asked the magic question that came from having worked with and dated doctors in the past.

"Not until Sunday."

Sunday. She'd be back in Atlanta by Saturday evening.

That meant they had two nights without interruption.

What was she thinking? Nights?

It wasn't as if she was going to spend those two nights with him. After all, she expected him to be angry when he learned about Ryan, but once he calmed down, surely he'd see why she'd made the choices she had.

She had to believe he'd understand. For Ryan's sake, if nothing else.

The waiter reappeared and left the bill on the table. Before Kimberly could pick it up, Daniel did.

"I'll pay."

His brow lifted. "Is this a business meal, then?"

She knew what he was asking. Knew that he was allowing her to define their current relationship before they went to her room, but they both knew they'd crossed that invisible line a long time ago. Nothing between them could ever be just business.

"No," she answered honestly. "Tonight was personal, but I'll still pay."

He dropped several notes onto the table. "How personal?"

Kimberly didn't squirm, although she might have if she'd thought it would help give her the strength to hold his gaze. "Tonight was about me and you."

"Because of the past?"

She shook her head and stared straight into his eyes and hoped he could see what was in her heart. Was terrified that he actually might.

"Because of right now."

CHAPTER EIGHT

DANIEL cocked his head toward Kimberly because he was worried that his ears had played tricks on him.

The anxious way she held his gaze, the nervous tilt to her mouth told him Kimberly just admitted to having feelings for him.

God, he wished he wasn't so tired. He was functioning on thirty-six hours without sleep. Not the first time he'd done it, and it certainly wouldn't be the last, but he hadn't slept well all week, thanks to a certain blonde refusing to let his mind have peace.

A smart man would go home, rest, and think long and hard before contemplating becoming involved with the only woman who'd ever broken his heart.

Yet looking at her hopeful expression there was no way he could walk away.

"Can we go to my room to talk, Daniel?"

Only a stupid man would turn down an invitation made by a woman like Kimberly.

Daniel wasn't stupid.

He stood, took her hand and lifted it to his mouth. He placed a soft kiss in the center of her palm. "Let's go."

Gulping, she stood and laced her fingers through his. Her hand trembled. "Daniel, this isn't an invitation for more. I…" She hesitated. "There's a lot that needs to be said before you and I can move forward."

She wanted to talk. She wanted to move forward. She wanted. He could hear her want in her voice. Despite his logical arguments on the reasons why it shouldn't, Daniel's hope built with every floor ding of the elevator.

By the time they reached the twenty-third floor his insides felt raw. Raw and ready and racing.

Logic stayed somewhere on the main level, and his libido had risen to the occasion.

Kimberly fumbled with her room key, sliding the card several times before the light blinked green.

Looking unsure, she flipped on the light, met his gaze, and took a deep breath. "There's so much I need to say to you that I don't even know where to begin."

She really wanted to talk? That's really why she'd invited him to her room? And why wasn't she shutting the door? She stood there, holding the door wide and looking ready to bolt.

She laughed nervously. "I— Do you want a drink? There's a minibar and—"

He didn't want to talk. "Shut the door, Kimberly."

"The door?" She glanced at where she held the door, blinked as if she hadn't realized she was still holding it open, and nodded. "Okay."

But she didn't.

She moistened her lips and lifted her eyes to his.

Tension zapped between them.

He took a step toward her, placed his hand over hers, and released her fingers from the door one by one.

The moment the door closed, Daniel pulled her to him, and their lips touched in a hungry kiss.

A hungry kiss that demanded more. A hungry kiss that released long-suppressed desires. A hungry kiss that threatened to devour his whole being.

He touched everywhere, feeling, caressing, refreshing his memory, learning the changes to her woman's body.

She was just as intent on rediscovering him. After skimming his shoulders and arms, she slid her hands down his back, causing every muscle to contract beneath her touch. Her fingers ran over his lower back, pulling him closer, burning him.

He kissed her throat, her neck, breathing in the scent that he'd never forgotten. Kimberly.

It was a fragrance that brought him home. Home to a place where only the two of them existed, where he needed what only she could provide, where he wanted nothing more than to give her the world.

At the moment she felt like all he'd ever wanted, ever needed.

"Kimberly," he groaned at the passion with which she kissed him. Like she was starved.

Not in his wildest fantasies had he thought this moment would happen.

Sure, he'd dreamed about it. Craved it.

That didn't mean he'd ever believed Kimberly would want him.

Then again, he'd never understood why she had suddenly quit wanting him all those years ago.

They'd gone from wonderful letters saying she couldn't wait for him to come home to her seeing someone else in just a few weeks of him leaving for medical school.

Struggling to meet the demands of his rigorous schedule and maintaining a job, he'd let her slip through his fingers.

He couldn't think about that right now.

Not when she responded so sweetly to the kisses he blazed over her skin.

Besides, it was in the past and the here and now was much more exciting.

He rapidly undid the buttons of his shirt and shucked the garment off his shoulders.

She watched him peel off the T-shirt he always wore beneath his shirt. Her eyes darkened with desire, making him want to give her everything, to stare into her eyes and see her pleasure when he made love to her.

She didn't comment when he removed her shirt, when he dropped kisses on her bare shoulders.

Slowly, he removed her slacks, and his, leaving them both standing in their underwear, just inside the hotel room entranceway.

Stepping back, she stared at him from head to toe. She drank in the sight of him and lifted dewy soft green eyes. "You're beautiful, Daniel."

He wanted to laugh, but the way she looked at him made him feel beautiful.

Which made him feel uneasy.

Men weren't supposed to feel beautiful, were they?

But her eyes ate him up, told him he was the sexiest man she'd ever seen, and most of all they said she wanted him every bit as much as he wanted her.

His gaze lowered to the silky lace covering her full breasts, larger, softer than they'd been at seventeen. "So are you."

She blushed.

"My body's changed," she warned, looking shy for the first time since they'd entered the room, like she wanted to cover herself, keep him from seeing the changes.

"For the better."

He meant it. She had the curves of a woman, not a young girl's body. Oh, he'd craved her enough back in the past, but now he wanted her with a man's lust, not that of a boy.

"Daniel." His name choked out of her mouth, and she moved into his arms. "There's so much I need to say to you before this happens."

Words would only get in their way. Besides, he didn't know what to say, how to put what he was feeling into words. Much better to show her.

Despite her soft protests, he lifted her, carried her to her king-sized bed, grateful she had a room with a bed big enough for both of them.

Ripping back the covers, he lowered her and, after sliding out of his underwear, he joined her between the crisp cream-colored sheets.

"We'll talk later, Kimberly. Let me touch you first. Please."

She hesitated, looked torn, which on some level told him they should talk first, but this was Kimberly. His Kimberly, and he'd missed her. For fifteen years he'd missed looking into her eyes, missed touching her and knowing she was his.

For the moment she was his again and he'd take the moment and make it his own.

"Daniel."

How many nights had he woken up over the years

with her sweet voice in his ear, calling out his name, only to find that he'd dreamed her yet again?

Tonight was no dream. This was real.

He and Kimberly, as they had always been meant to be. Together.

He kissed her. Long and hard and until they were both breathless. Then he kissed her more. Her lips. Her pretty face. Her soft throat. Her breasts.

He kissed her until she whimpered beneath him, held on to his shoulders and met his gaze with such longing and need he could no longer restrain himself.

Until he no longer wanted anything but Kimberly.

He slipped her panties down her hips.

"I want you," he whispered, sliding his hands over her, inside her. He stroked, lavished her with attention, soaked up the caresses she bestowed on his aching body.

A voice deep within screamed that this was Kimberly he held, Kimberly he touched, and had he lost his mind?

"Daniel, please," she whispered against his lips, her gaze locked on his. What he saw in her eyes told him he had lost his mind. Had lost his mind the moment he'd met her and had never regained it.

Hating to get up, he did so, found his wallet and got out a condom.

In seconds he had the rubber barrier rolled over himself.

One thrust of his hips brought him deep into where he always wanted to be. Where he never wanted to leave.

"Kimberly."

She was tight and hot and wet.

He wasn't going to last.

But he paced himself, moving slowly at first, watching her eyes glaze with passion, feeling her body wind tighter and tighter as she neared orgasm.

"I've missed you, Daniel. So much."

Somewhere in the back of his mind he wanted to remind her he'd wanted to spend his life loving her and she'd been the one to walk away from their relationship.

"Tell me," he encouraged her, wanting to hear her words of need, wanting to know he wasn't alone in this crazy need.

The rhythm between them spiraled upward, steadily building to a crescendo, steadily engulfing more and more of reality and carrying them to some other world where only the two of them existed.

"I dream of you," she panted into his ear, her voice a raspy whisper. "I wake up with thoughts of you haunting my mind, my body."

He kissed her deeply.

Knowing she was on the brink, he held back his own release only with the greatest willpower.

"What do I do in these dreams?" he asked, immersing himself inside her in a slow, torturous stroke that would certainly haunt his own dreams for years.

"You love me, Daniel." Her fists clenched and unclenched in the sheets, then she drew him close, holding him to her, and greedily demanded he love her at this very moment.

Whatever willpower he'd thought he held evaporated and his tempo picked up, driving them toward the pleasurable burst they sought.

He felt her orgasm, felt her flesh tighten, spasm around him.

"In my dreams…" Her words came out in short gasps

as her body worked in rhythm with his, reaching higher and higher. "You loved me."

Her nails dug in, her back arched, and she moaned beneath him.

"Now," she pleaded. "Love me, now, Daniel. Please, please, love me."

He did.

Kimberly couldn't say it surprised her when Daniel fell asleep almost immediately afterward.

At first she'd thought he had only been resting, but his even breathing and soft snores told the real story.

He'd made love to her and dozed off.

Under different circumstances she might have been offended, hurt even, but Daniel needed sleep, and she cherished the opportunity to openly study his features.

Laughter lines fanned out from the corners of his eyes and fine creases marred his forehead, but they only added to his appeal, giving character and strength to his handsome face. His nose still slanted proudly and his mouth should come with a warning that touching caused explosive reactions.

His hands should carry a similar warning because everywhere he'd touched she'd exploded with the most wicked of sensations.

No one had ever made her feel like Daniel did.

Not even her ex-husband. She'd cared for Thomas. She wouldn't have married him if she hadn't, but their friendship hadn't laid the foundation to build on that they'd hoped for. Thomas had remarried and had two small kids. Kimberly couldn't be happier for him because he was a good man.

Just not the man for her.

Gently, she stroked her fingertip over Daniel's face.

"I love you," she whispered, knowing he was sound asleep and would never know her admission. "I've always loved you, and I always will."

He never acknowledged her words in any way, neither did she expect him to miraculously wake up and shout with glee.

Just lying next to him, with his arm draped over her, his breath on her cheek, and the ability to watch him sleep was enough.

"We have a son, Daniel. A gorgeous son who is so much like you. I'm going to tell you all about him. Soon." She pressed a soft kiss to his lips. "Please, understand."

Daniel felt more rested than he had in a very long time. He stretched languidly. Realizing a warm body snuggled against him, he remembered the night's events.

Kimberly.

His heart raced at the ramifications of what they'd shared.

Technically, nothing they hadn't shared before, yet so much more.

Last night had been different. More intense than anything their teenage bodies had experienced. More real.

She'd asked him to love her.

Had she been speaking in physical terms? Or metaphorically? Did she want more than just the fabulous sex they'd shared?

He hoped so, because no way was he letting her walk away at the end of the week. Tomorrow.

He'd let her slip from his life once. All that had given

him was fifteen years of unfavorably comparing every woman he'd met to her.

This time, if she tried, he wouldn't let her push him away. Not without a fight.

He should have fought for her a long time ago, but he'd been eighteen. What had he known at the time about life and how precious having someone you cared about at your side was?

Remembering how he'd loved her, he decided maybe he'd known more than he was giving himself credit for. What he hadn't known was how wrong he'd been to let her move on to some other guy. It should have been him she'd married, his child she'd given birth to.

He leaned forward, brushed his nose against her long blond tresses and breathed in her scent, filling his heart and mind with the fragrance that was solely Kimberly.

His body stirred, hardening at just that single stimulus. Amazing how something so simple could bring him from zero to sixty in a second when other women had failed to move him for so long.

Because he wanted more.

He wanted a relationship and commitment.

He wanted Kimberly.

Her naked body was spooned against his in an enticing fashion. Dropping soft kisses against the back of her neck, he snaked his hand out to finger her breasts, slowly caressing, slowly waking her body to the morning and to him.

She moaned softly, shifting against his body. Rousing, she twisted and fluttered her lashes. Her hair was tousled sexily about her face and a sleepy, unsure smile played on her lips.

"You're up."

"Literally."

Pink tinged her cheeks.

"Daniel," she scolded, the uneasiness in her eyes replaced with delighted mischief, and he laughed, loving it that he'd made her smile, given her happiness.

"Good morning, sunshine."

No matter how long he'd denied it, Kimberly was his dream woman.

"Oh, Daniel." Her smile fading, she inhaled audibly. "What have we done?"

Not what he wanted to hear.

"We need to slow down. We should talk before anything else happens between us." She winced. "We should have talked before anything happened last night."

"We can talk later." Because he really didn't want her overanalyzing everything that had happened between them during the past twenty-four hours.

"I'm serious." She pushed against his chest, making him listen. "I have to tell you something."

He sighed. Was it wrong that he just wanted to feel what was between them and not put it into words? Words would only mar the perfection of when their bodies connected, and didn't actions speak louder than words anyway?

"If you insist on talking, let's shower and have breakfast first." He knew he sounded grumpy, but he already knew what he needed to know.

They were starting over and he'd convince her that being together was right.

"But first I want a good-morning kiss." He smacked his lips to hers in a playful kiss, determined to keep the mood light between them. "Ah, come on. You can do better than that," he teased when she resisted.

"Daniel!" She swatted at him, but then he went for another kiss and another and her hands quit their flapping and welcomed him.

One touch led to another and then another until they were clamoring for each other and his body strained for release.

He rolled over to reach for his wallet to get a condom, and found the night table bare except for the standard hotel clock and lamp. Frowning, he felt on the floor to see if they'd knocked his wallet off during the night and found it.

Unfortunately, he didn't find another condom.

CHAPTER NINE

KIMBERLY stared across the hospital cafeteria table and wondered how she could have been so stupid.

She'd had sex with Daniel without telling him about Ryan. Admittedly telling him about Ryan would have killed the desire to have sex, but she should have told him before they'd slept together.

Slept together.

Something they hadn't ever done. Sure, they'd taken short naps after making love, but they'd never slept in a bed all night together.

He'd kept his arm draped around her protectively and at one point during the night she'd woken up, realized she lay next to Daniel and cried.

Lying in his arms, waking up next to him, it's what she'd wanted for so long.

That morning, when he'd caught her misty-eyed and had wanted to know what was wrong, she hadn't been able to tell him the truth, not when it would have meant erasing the warmth from his eyes, not when it would have meant replacing his smile with a frown, and losing whatever it was between them.

But her heart pricked and she couldn't bear it any longer.

"You okay?" Daniel asked, downing half his glass of orange juice in a single drink.

"Fine," she lied.

It seemed she was born to deceive this man. Odd, as he mattered so much to her and she was generally an honest person.

She was tired of lying to Daniel.

Tired of the secrets between them.

She wanted Daniel in her life, wanted him to know Ryan and to love their son the way she did.

"What are you thinking about?" Daniel's eyes pierced her thoughts.

No more lies.

"This morning." He'd been upset when he'd realized they hadn't had any protection, but had given her release with his mouth and hands.

"I'll make it up to you tonight," he promised. "Apparently neither of us was prepared for a night of sex."

"No," she admitted, not meeting his eyes.

"You regret what happened?"

"It was inevitable, I suppose."

"Inevitable?" He frowned. "You make it sound like a disease."

"We should have talked before sleeping together, Daniel."

"Weren't you listening, Kimberly?" His voice was low, seductive, making her cheeks flush with heat. "My body was telling you everything."

How did they get onto this topic while in the hospital cafeteria?

Fortunately, the closest people to them were two older women sipping coffee and unaware of the tension four tables over.

Daniel took her hand in his. "Just as your body told me everything I needed to know."

Heat flushed her face. "What is it that you think my body told you?"

"That you still have feelings for me."

She didn't deny it.

"That we're good together."

She couldn't deny that either.

"I think we should give it another go, Kimberly."

"Another go?" She blinked at him. What was he saying? Why did her blood slam through her body, causing dizziness to swamp her?

"As in have a relationship."

"You want a relationship with me?"

"Yes."

"I live in Atlanta."

He studied her a minute, then squeezed her hand. "Frequent flyer programs were created for couples like us."

He wanted to maintain a long-distance relationship? To come to Atlanta to spend time with her?

"You'd fly to Atlanta to be with me?"

"I'd paddle to Africa to be with you."

Kimberly smiled. She couldn't help it. He looked and sounded so sincere.

"You expect me to believe you when all this time all you had to do was make a trip home to Atlanta? I've been there all along, Daniel. You were the one who stayed gone."

"You told me to leave and never come back."

Because of our son.

"Right or wrong, I did what I thought was right at the time," she said slowly, her thoughts heavy on her mind.

"But you still cared about me?" His eyes searched hers. "Even then, you cared?"

"I loved you."

A pained look swept across his face. "You broke my heart, Kimberly."

"I'd never hurt you intentionally, Daniel." Another lie because she had hurt him intentionally when she'd broken things off. She'd hurt him so he could move on with his life, his dreams.

She gulped, knowing what she had to do. What she'd meant to do when she'd invited him to her room but had been sidetracked, had wanted to be sidetracked, if truth be told. She'd wanted one night with him before all hell broke loose.

Delaying only made things worse, made her secret weigh more heavily upon her heart.

Besides, telling him in private might be impossible after last night.

If she were alone with Daniel she'd likely be ripping off his clothes.

"Actually, that's not true," she corrected herself, causing his gaze to shoot to her. She sought the right words, words that would convey how she'd struggled with the burden she'd carried alone that fall. "I'd never want to hurt you, Daniel, but sometimes difficult choices have to be made and someone you never meant to hurt does get hurt."

His eyes narrowed. "You're talking about when we broke up?"

"Yes." She nodded, willing her heartbeat to remain steady, for her focus to remain intact, because Daniel had a right to know his son. "I'm talking about when I had a difficult choice to make and you got hurt in the process."

Confusion distorted his handsome face and he gave her a blank look. "The choice being me, who you claim you still loved, and this other guy you left me for?"

"There wasn't another guy. At least, not in the sense you mean." She opened her mouth to tell him about Ryan, but his pager buzzed to life.

His gaze held hers for three seconds, then he glanced at the number and cursed. "A patient just went into code blue. Got to go."

His gaze landed on the tray of half-eaten food in front of him.

"I'll take care of it."

"Thanks, Kimberly." He paused long enough to meet her eyes. "I'll see you later. Greg is doing a couple of procedures this morning. If I'm not in my office by eight, have Trina page him so you can observe. I'll find you when I can."

He bent and did something she suspected was totally out of character. He kissed the top of her head.

Nothing sexual, just a tender kiss that said he cared and wanted her to know.

"We'll talk tonight and figure out a way to make this work because we're worth giving a chance to."

She nodded, watching as he rushed out of the cafeteria, wishing she'd had the opportunity to tell him about Ryan yet grateful she hadn't blurted it out because he'd received the page.

Daniel didn't need fatherhood distracting him while someone's life rested in his hands.

Or was that just an excuse for delaying the hatred she knew was sure to come with the truth?

They were worth giving a chance to, and that's exactly what she'd never allowed them.

That evening, Kimberly sat in Daniel's office, waiting for him to return. He'd let her use his computer to log on to her Cardico account and electronically sign off on work regarding her week in Boston.

She could have done so later that evening or even tomorrow, but he'd had a staff meeting that had given her an odd hour while she'd finished her training on the CRT pacemaker.

What an amazing device and what an amazing doctor.

His colleagues admired him for much more than just his skills with the ladies. During the week she'd watched doctors from various fields consult him. Daniel had always given an intelligent, thoughtful answer.

She really was proud of all he'd accomplished.

They were worth giving a chance to.

Had last night changed that much? If he hadn't fallen asleep, would they have talked? Lain in each other's arms and revealed their hearts' secrets?

What was in Daniel's heart?

He'd said he wanted a relationship, but did he really mean that he wanted sex until he lost interest?

Would she ultimately be just another notch in his bedpost?

No, she didn't believe that.

Daniel hadn't been a ladies' man back when they'd been together.

He'd been hers.

In every way that counted.

In none of the ways that counted.

Hadn't it been easy for Leona to convince her that she was nothing more than a casual fling to Daniel? That she'd ruin his life if she forced her "brat" on him? If she loved Daniel so much, how could she rob him of his dreams?

Ultimately, she hadn't been able to tell him so she'd broken up with him over the Christmas holidays with the story that she'd met someone while he'd been away.

And after minimal fuss he'd believed her and flown back to Boston.

She wouldn't go home until Daniel knew the truth. The truth she'd been too young, scared and insecure to tell him fifteen years ago.

No matter what the consequences, she'd make the right choice this time and let Daniel choose the role he would play in her and Ryan's lives.

She logged out of her account, glanced at the time on the right of the computer screen and wondered what to do to fill the remainder of her wait.

Maybe she could watch the clip on the CRT again that Gregory had pulled up on Monday.

Or play that game of solitaire.

She clicked on the start icon, which pulled up the menu. Aha. Solitaire. She moved the cursor over the game, but was distracted by a folder labeled "My Photos."

He probably didn't even have any photos and it was just something that had come with the computer.

She had no right to pry. None whatsoever.

Yet the cursor slid over to "My Photos." And clicked, which started an obviously preprogrammed slide show.

Daniel did have photos. Apparently, he'd recently

taken a trip out to the Grand Canyon and had some amazing shots.

Some not so amazing ones of him with a skinny blonde who'd also gone on the trip.

There were a couple of ski trips to Boulder. Group holidays—she recognized several of the doctors Daniel worked with, including Greg.

A different blonde accompanied Daniel on each trip.

Jealousy clenched her heart and she had to remind herself that she had no right to be jealous of anything in Daniel's past.

Telling herself and convincing herself were two different things.

She moved the mouse, intending to close the file, but when she moved the cursor it closed the slide show and pulled up his photo folders.

One was marked "Home."

She bit the inside of her lip, feeling criminal for prying through his personal photos, yet her curiosity was too strong not to want to see where Daniel lived.

Only it wasn't photos of his current home that came up. It was a snapshot of him and his mom standing in front of their Georgia home and one of her sitting on the trunk of his car only weeks before she'd discovered she was pregnant.

Memories flooded her. The hot metal of his car had burned through her thin cotton shorts. There had been a light breeze, which explained why her hair had a bit of a flyaway look. But she looked happier than she recalled ever being.

Her eyes practically glowed with amusement and her mouth turned upward in a half smile, half pout. She recalled that she'd been teasing Daniel to put away the camera and come and kiss her.

He'd done much more than that.

"About finished?" Daniel asked, entering the office with a stack of papers.

Kimberly clicked to close the photos so quickly that Daniel had to see her guilt. But he only dropped the papers onto his desk and grinned.

"You spying for secrets to sell Cardico?"

"No," she gasped, shocked at his question, but more appalled at herself because she had been spying. For herself rather than for her company.

"I'm teasing, Kimberly." He reached out and ran his finger over her cheek. "You really need to relax."

"Tomorrow," she said, still reeling from her guilt at prying on his computer and from the fact that he'd been totally businesslike since that morning and now he was touching her.

"Tomorrow?"

"I fly home late tomorrow afternoon. I'll relax then."

"Hmm." Surprisingly, he didn't say more. She'd hoped to spend her time with him, but maybe he wouldn't have anyway once she told him about Ryan.

"You ready to make rounds? Then we'll go out to celebrate the end of your training."

"It's not really the end." She was observing three CRT pacemaker placements in the morning.

"Semantics."

"Thanks again for letting me use the computer." *Sorry, I pried into your pictures.* "I got most of my work done."

"Great. You can't use that as an excuse not to go with me tonight."

"You think I'd make excuses not to go out with you after last night, Daniel?"

"Something's bothering you. Has been all day." He read her too easily. "I thought you might be having regrets about last night. Or about me pushing you for more this morning," he added sheepishly. "I know things are moving fast, but it's not like we were strangers to begin with."

"I'm not upset at you about this morning." How could she be when if it hadn't been for the secrets between them she'd be ecstatic at the prospect of starting over with Daniel?

"I'm glad." He took her hand and pulled her to her feet. "Let's go make rounds so we can get out of here."

CHAPTER TEN

"I'VE been with Cardico for almost five years," Kimberly said, stuffing a shrimp into her mouth. "I took the position after working for a pharmaceutical company for a couple of years. I pushed a blood-pressure medicine that I believed to be superior to its competitors, but my products changed and so did my love of my job."

They'd finished at the hospital, and although she wouldn't have been averse to heading straight back to her hotel room so she could tell him about Ryan, they were at a place called Bubba Joe's Seafood, an out-of-the-way, rough-looking pub that he'd sworn had the best seafood in all of Boston.

From what she'd sampled, she agreed.

"But you started out as a cardiology nurse?" Daniel asked. He leaned back against the cheap vinyl cushioning of the booth and took a sip of his beer.

Kimberly's gaze zeroed in on where his lips met the glass bottle. She closed her eyes and for a brief moment imagined those lips next to hers as they'd been last night, this morning.

"I worked on the cardiology unit for five years."

"Where did you do your nursing training?"

She told him the name of a local community program. "I went for an associate's degree in a two-year program." She'd had a baby to take care of. "After I earned my degree, I enrolled in a bachelor's program and earned my BSN."

"Why didn't you go straight for your Bachelor of Science?"

"I worked full-time from the moment I graduated from high school. Earning my associate degree first enabled me to gain experience while providing a better living for Ryan and me."

His forehead furrowed. "You got pregnant before college?"

Kimberly choked on the shrimp she'd just popped into her mouth and coughed to clear her throat.

Daniel slapped her back, trying to help her catch her breath.

She took a long drink of her beer, more to stall than to wash down any remaining food.

She'd wanted to tell him last night and again this morning, but it hadn't happened. Last night Daniel had been tired and they'd been distracted by lust. Daniel wasn't on call tonight and they had the entire night ahead of them, with only a few patients in the morning.

Now's the time. Tell him about Ryan. Tell him that he has a gorgeous, wonderful fourteen-year-old son.

Seeming to sense her thoughts, he took her hand and lowered his voice to a soft, seductive purr.

"Tell me about your son, Kimberly. I've not asked much about him because I wasn't sure I wanted to hear about someone else's kid, but I do for the simple reason

that everything to do with you interests me." He inter-
laced their fingers. "How old is he? What's he like?
Does he look like you?"

"He looks like his father." She needed something
stronger than beer to drink. Much stronger.

"Your ex-husband?"

She shook her head. "No, Ryan was three when I
married Thomas."

Daniel looked taken aback.

"He worked in administration at the hospital where
I worked while earning my BSN," she explained. "I
didn't trick him in any way. He knew I loved my baby's
father very much and despite the time that had passed,
I was still on the rebound in many ways."

Too many ways. She'd been scared and trying to figure
out her life when Thomas had come along. His friendship
had offered her hope and she'd desperately taken it.

"Ryan's father left you?" Daniel sounded incredulous.

"He didn't have a choice."

"There's always a choice," he snorted, disbelief
written all over his face.

This wasn't the lead-in she'd hoped for to tell him
about Ryan. Maybe there wasn't a good lead-in.

"Sometimes life's choices aren't easy ones and a
person has to do what they think is right."

"He thought leaving you to raise a baby by yourself
was the right choice?" He shook his head. "He didn't
deserve you."

She closed her eyes, prayed her eardrums wouldn't
burst from the loud roaring of her heartbeat. She had to
tell him, right now.

"Daniel—" she began.

"It's none of my business, right?" He smiled wryly, turned her hand in his and traced her lifeline. "You know, I wasn't sure how I felt when I saw you on Monday morning. But I'm glad you came to Boston, Kimberly. Glad our paths crossed again."

He lifted her palm and kissed the center. "Very glad."

"Daniel, I need to tell you something."

Her tone must have warned that what she had to say was serious, because he squeezed her hand. "Tell me."

"When I told you that Ryan doesn't look like me, that he looks like his father, well, there was more to it. About his father, I mean."

He winced. "I don't want to hear about this guy. What's in the past is in the past. Ryan's father no longer matters."

"He does. I need you to understand why I made the choices I did."

He regarded her, his eyes dark and unreadable. "Okay, tell me."

"I loved Ryan's father."

"You've already said that," he interrupted, shaking his head. "You're talking in circles."

Frustrated, she glanced around the noisy restaurant. Maybe telling him that he was a father while in the middle of a boisterous pub wasn't such a good idea, but the moment pressed urgently, and she had to tell him. Right now, before she found an excuse not to.

"You're Ryan's father."

His hand fell away from hers and he stared at her, his eyes narrowed. "What did you say?"

"You're Ryan's father."

He shook his head as if to clear it. "I didn't hear you. Tell me again."

She took a deep breath and started over. "I was pregnant when I broke up with you, Daniel. You're Ryan's father."

Stunned didn't begin to describe the look on his face. "You're sure?"

"Positive, Daniel." She smiled softly. "Every time I look at him, I see you in his eyes, his smile, the way he carries himself. He's your image."

"I have a son?" His face pulled tight and dazed eyes stared at her, but she wasn't sure they saw.

Fighting the panic in her belly, she nodded. "Ryan's fourteen."

"Fourteen?"

She nodded. "He'll be fifteen in April."

"I have a son who's almost fifteen and you're only now telling me?" Daniel snapped out of his shocked haze and glared. His fist came down hard on the thick wooden table, sending bottles toppling.

Wincing at his anger, Kimberly scurried to straighten them before anything spilled. "Daniel, please."

"Please?" he mocked. "Please, what? Please, ignore the fact that you're telling me I have a son who's almost grown up and I've missed out on his entire life?"

"It's not like that," she began, but Daniel had a point. It *was* like that.

That's exactly what she'd cheated him out of for fourteen years.

Sure, her reasons had started out noble, but she had to face the truth.

Fear of losing Ryan the way she'd lost Daniel was the only reason her son didn't know his father, was the only reason Daniel didn't know his son.

After Daniel had graduated from medical school she should have gone to him, told him the truth, begged him to forgive her and still love her. But time had passed and she'd been afraid. Afraid of rejection. Afraid of losing Ryan.

Afraid of not being good enough.

Even now, fear besieged her. Fear of how Ryan would take this, but even more, fear of the hatred she saw blazing in Daniel's eyes.

Hatred she understood because she'd have felt it herself if someone had told her she'd had to give up the last fourteen years with her son.

"I'm sorry, Daniel. I made the choice I thought was right."

"The right choice?" he scoffed, his breath coming out in heavy puffs, his jaw flexing. "You had my baby and didn't tell me. How is that the right choice?"

When he put it like that, her thought process was difficult to recall. But she had believed it to be the right choice.

So had his mother.

Leona had begged her not to tell Daniel, to have an abortion, and let Daniel have his dream.

She'd even given Kimberly money to pay for the procedure.

For all she knew, Leona believed she'd had an abortion because she'd not spoken to the woman since breaking things off with Daniel.

Then again, if Leona had read her mother's obituary last year, she would have seen Ryan listed as having survived his grandmother. At the very least, Leona had to have wondered about Ryan.

All she would have had to do was pick up the sports section to see article after article mentioning Ryan.

"I'm not perfect," she began, battling memories of just how imperfect she'd felt when confronted by his mother. "But I truly did what I thought right."

She reached out to touch him, but he jerked away.

Tears rolled down her cheeks and she fought to keep from running out of the restaurant. Running back to Atlanta and the comfort of her carefully orchestrated life.

"Daniel, no matter what you think, I never meant to hurt you. I was only seventeen, and I was scared." God, she'd been scared. Scared of being so young, of having to tell her mother, having to face her senior year of high school while pregnant, having to face the rest of her life as a single mom, but she'd done it. "I made the best decision I could at the time."

He stared at her, his teeth gritted, his hands clenched, his body tight with tension.

When his eyes closed, she noticed the bulging vein at his temple, the rapid beat jumping, showing just how much he strained to hold in his wrath.

When he opened his eyes, he seemed to have reached decisions, and he motioned for the waiter. "We're leaving."

Unsure what to say, she nodded.

The waiter brought their bill and Daniel dropped money onto the table. "Let's get out of here."

He took her hand, but in more of a viselike grip than the tender caress of earlier. Without a word, he led her around crowded tables toward the front of the restaurant.

A commotion a few tables over caught her eye about the same time as it caught Daniel's.

A morbidly obese man slid out of his chair and onto the wooden-planked floor. A young boy and woman also sat at the table.

"Ken?" the woman screeched, jumping out of her seat and going around to where the man lay still. "Oh, my God, someone call 911. My husband's passed out."

The little boy's face turned white. He dropped to his knees and began tugging on the man's straining shirt. "Daddy, wake up. Daddy, you aren't supposed to lie down in the food place. Daddy, please, wake up."

Daniel and Kimberly exchanged a lightning-fast look. Setting their private concerns aside, they headed to where the man lay. A crowd had already started to gather.

"I'm a doctor," Daniel announced, pushing his way through the onlookers. "Please, step back so I have room to check him and he has room to breathe."

Daniel did the ABCs of first aid. Airway. Breathing. Circulation. From the look on his face, Kimberly could tell he didn't like what he found.

And that the little boy's tears were getting to him.

Because she'd told him about Ryan? Because he'd missed out on seeing Ryan at that age? Because if he'd died, Ryan would never have known him, and vice versa.

She'd cheated him out of so much.

She sank her teeth into her lower lip to hold in a cry full of regret.

"No pulse," Daniel told her, grimacing, though whether at her or the man she wasn't sure. He loosened the man's clothing in a quick yank that popped the straining buttons and started chest compressions. "I think he's had a heart attack."

"My mouth guard's in my purse," Kimberly told him, stopping him from doing mouth to mouth unprotected, although he'd been going to do so without hesitation, with no regard to his own health.

Daniel nodded, taking over the compressions so she could find the guard.

Not wanting to waste precious time searching through her cluttered bag, she dumped the entire contents of her purse on the floor and grabbed the Cellophane-sealed mouthpiece that prevented the exchange of germs, including if the man vomited, which sometimes happened.

Putting it on, she bent and blew a breath into the man's mouth. Due to his large size, she honestly couldn't tell if his lungs expanded or not, but she knew Daniel would tell her if she wasn't profusing them with air.

Keeping in rhythm with Daniel, she gave a breath to every five of his compressions.

"He's only forty. He can't be having a heart attack." The man's wife wobbled. "Men don't have heart attacks at forty."

Unfortunately they did.

Kimberly motioned for a bystander to help the woman into a chair and for the little boy to join his mother, but he shook his head, glaring at Daniel.

"My daddy's just sleeping." Panic lifted his young voice to a high pitch. "He's just sleeping."

His face tightly controlled, Daniel ignored the boy and glanced at a frozen-to-the-spot waiter. "Call 911, and request an ambulance. *Now.*"

His eyes giving the lifeless man one last look, the waiter rushed toward the front of the restaurant, presumably where he'd make the call.

In between giving breaths, her gaze met Daniel's.

He nodded at her unspoken question.

Without missing a compression, she relieved him and began counting in her head as she used pent-up frustration to give her the strength to press hard against the man's huge chest over and over in a synchronized rhythm.

"Does anyone have any nitroglycerin?"

The little boy's eyes went round. "You're not blowing up my daddy!"

Daniel's gaze touched on the boy for a split second, but he didn't comment, just took a tiny brown medicine bottle from a fifty-ish man who stood watching and who looked quite pale.

In between blowing air into the man's lungs, Daniel turned to the heart attack patient's wife. "Is he on any medications? Or does he have any known health problems?"

"His cholesterol, but that's it. He's as healthy as a horse."

"No Viagra, Levitra, or Cialis?"

The woman looked appalled, and gave her son a blushing glance. "Of course not."

Kimberly continued to compress, and Daniel placed a small white tablet under the man's tongue. The medication would dissolve on its own and cause the blood vessels to dilate, allowing more easy passage of blood to vital parts.

The moment he'd done so he motioned for her to change spots and she readily did so, taking over giving the man air in sync with Daniel's compressions.

CPR was hard work. Anyone who hadn't performed

it had no idea of the stamina required to keep at it, of the strain it took on a person.

After what seemed like hours, but couldn't have been more than a few minutes at most, Kimberly offered to trade, to give Daniel a break, but he shook his head.

That's when she saw it.

The way he kept glancing at the little boy, who was sobbing in his mother's arms.

She knew what he was thinking, what he was remembering.

Not about Ryan, but the day his father had died.

How his own mother had held him while he'd cried.

He'd already been kicked in the gut by her revelation about Ryan. Being subjected to this, to the memories it would bring back, might down him.

Never had she wanted to hold him more, to take him in her arms and love away his worries. Or at least do her best to try.

Daniel's pain was her pain and she'd caused so much of the hurt he'd experienced tonight. Although nothing could atone for what she'd done, she'd spend the rest of her life attempting to make up for what she'd robbed him of.

Never had Kimberly been so relieved as when she heard the wail of the ambulance's sirens.

The paramedics quickly took over, injecting the man with atropine and shocking him with a mobile defibrillator. And again.

"We have a heartbeat!" one of the paramedics exclaimed, and a cheer went up from the crowd.

Not that the man was out of danger, but the fact he now had a heartbeat gave better odds of survival.

The man's size made transport difficult and every second could mean the difference between life or death. The paramedics placed him on the stretcher and rolled him out to the ambulance.

The man's wife had gone into shock and his son flew into hysterics. He screamed and cried after the paramedics.

"Don't take my daddy. Please, don't take my daddy. I've got to wake him up."

He took off after the stretcher and, fighting tears, Kimberly wrapped her arms around his small body. He couldn't be more than six or seven at most.

"Shh, they're taking him to the hospital so they can care for him," she whispered against his soft hair. "You've got to stay with your mom. She needs you to take care of her right now."

"I need to go with my daddy. I have to wake him up."

"I don't think I can drive," the woman cried, her voice breaking. "I'm shaking, and I don't think I can drive. What if I crash?"

She looked at Kimberly in desperation.

"Kimberly will drive you and your son in my car, and I'll lead the way in yours," Daniel said, coming back to where they were after he'd helped the paramedics with the man. "That way you'll have your car when you're ready to leave the hospital."

Kimberly nodded, still holding the young boy in her arms and trying not to let tears flow at the stony detachment on Daniel's face.

But when he looked at her, met her gaze, the utter loss in his eyes undid her resolve and moisture stung her cheeks.

Oh, Daniel.

Looking numb, the woman nodded.

"Let's go." He turned and headed back out of the restaurant, ignoring the cheers and backslaps that the other patrons gave him for what he'd done for the man.

Kimberly watched him go, clutching the trembling little boy to her the way she wanted to hold Daniel, to comfort his losses.

Only she knew he'd shrug away any attempts she made to comfort him. He'd only ever talked about his dad on one occasion and that had been brief.

It had been Leona who'd told her how Daniel's father had died, how it had affected Daniel, why it was so important that he fulfill his dreams of becoming a cardiologist.

On a daily basis Daniel faced his demons in the sterile setting of the hospital and he kept them tightly in check.

But here, in a restaurant with an innocent little boy watching, Daniel hadn't been able to control those repressed emotions.

The little boy gulped a deep breath, reminding Kimberly that, as much as she longed to go to Daniel, she had others to take care of at the moment.

"I'm Kimberly Brookes," she introduced herself to the boy and his mother, keeping her voice calm, soothing. "I'm a registered nurse. And that—" her gaze went to where Daniel rounded the corner of the entranceway "—is Dr. Daniel Travis."

"Beverly Reynolds," the woman said, shakily getting to her feet and wrapping her arms around her son. "And this is Devon."

"He's a hero, ma'am. A real-life hero," the waiter

who'd called for the ambulance announced, earning several bellows of agreement from the crowd.

"Yes," Kimberly agreed, "he is."

Daniel had always been the hero of her heart.

Daniel raked a hand through his hair and leaned against the wall outside the operating room where Greg was performing open-heart surgery on Ken Reynolds.

His partner had asked if he'd wanted to come in and help with the procedure. Daniel had declined.

Because of fear.

Because of the sickness churning in the pit of his stomach.

Because he was a coward and couldn't face the monitor if the man's heart stopped again.

Even though the man's heart started beating after the paramedics had administered the electrical shocks, Mr. Reynolds wasn't out of the woods. If he made it through surgery, who knew what kind of damage had occurred to his brain and body during the time he'd technically been dead?

Brain damage could occur with even a small amount of oxygen deprivation.

And now, when the man was in surgery and there was nothing to keep Daniel from going out to the waiting room, he couldn't go.

Couldn't face the boy.

His mother.

Kimberly.

Especially Kimberly.

Because he'd seen the look in her eyes.

She'd known exactly what he'd thought.

That scared the hell out of him.

How could she have been pregnant, had his baby, and not told him?

Just because she'd dumped him, it didn't mean he'd have turned his back on her when she'd discovered she was pregnant. Had she really thought he'd not care? That he wouldn't have chosen to stay by her side and raise their child in lieu of coming to Boston? Or, better yet, he would have figured out a way to bring her with him. It might have meant giving up his scholarship, but he'd have found a way.

He had a son. A child. A baby.

Not a baby.

A fourteen-year-old.

A son he'd never seen. Never held. Never touched.

A son who wouldn't recognize his own father.

Damn her.

Damn her for what she'd stolen from him.

All the memories he'd never have of things like first words, first steps, first days of school, first baseball games. All gone. All beyond his ability of ever knowing, ever experiencing.

How could she have done that to him?

He'd not thought it possible, but in that moment he hated Kimberly.

Hated her for what she'd taken and selfishly kept for herself.

"Dr. Travis?" A cardiac nurse tapped him on the shoulder. "Dr. Jessup asked me to check on you. He said you were feeling poorly. Do you need me to get you anything?"

Her smile was friendly, concerned.

Feeling poorly? Greg had no idea.

Daniel shook his head. "Tell him I'm fine and that I'll be in my office. When he's finished with Ken Reynolds, have him let me know."

CHAPTER ELEVEN

KIMBERLY'S heart went out to Beverly Reynolds and how lost she must be, not knowing if her husband would live or not. The pale woman paced back and forth across the waiting room.

A nurse had come out not long after they'd arrived at the hospital to tell them Ken had been taken into the operating room. That's the last they'd heard and it seemed like a long time ago.

Kimberly's legs had gone numb about an hour ago, but Devon slept half on her lap, half sprawled across the sofa. He'd cried himself to sleep, and she didn't have the heart to risk waking him to restore circulation to her legs.

Tenderly, she stroked his hair, thinking it looked and felt much as Ryan's had at six.

At the moment, more than ever, she missed her son.

A son who was so like his father that her heart ached at times just from looking at him and the feeling of loss it evoked.

When she returned to Atlanta, that feeling would be tenfold because she'd seen the hurt in Daniel's eyes and she'd felt his pain, felt what she'd robbed him of and that she could never give back.

He wouldn't forgive her.

The waiting-room door opened.

"Nurse?" Beverly stilled, her hands wringing tightly as she waited for some word on her husband's condition.

Blinking, Kimberly's eyes shot to the uniformed woman standing in the entrance of the waiting room.

She winced at the worried look on the nurse's face.

Oh, no, had Mr. Reynolds died?

"My husband, how is he?" Beverly pleaded, looking at the nurse with hope. "Please, tell me he's okay."

"He's still in surgery. I'm sorry I can't tell you more." The nurse then turned to Kimberly. "You're Kimberly Brookes?"

She nodded.

"Can you, please, come with me?"

Her heart flopped. What had happened? Why would they want her?

Daniel.

She eased out from under the sleeping boy, grateful he didn't wake up as it might be hours before they'd know anything on his father and she hated the thought of having to look into his soulful brown eyes and not have good news.

Beverly grabbed her hand, held on tightly, panic in her eyes. "Please, come back and tell me if you learn anything on Ken. Promise me."

Kimberly nodded. "I promise."

Once outside the waiting room, the nurse gave her an awkward smile. "I have a message for you."

"For me?" *It had to be from Daniel.*

"Actually," the nurse continued, looking a bit sheepish, "I have two."

"Is Dr. Travis in surgery?" Perhaps he was doing Mr. Reynolds's bypass and was sending word to let her know he'd be a while.

"No, but one of the messages is from him. He wanted me to tell you to get a taxi back to your hotel. He's staying at the hospital tonight and will see you in the morning in the cardiac lab."

Disappointment spread through her. She'd be home tomorrow evening and had hoped for time with Daniel tonight for them to discuss Ryan, time to make him understand how she'd felt when he'd left for Boston.

"Okay," she told the nurse. "But I'm not leaving until I know how Mr. Reynolds is."

Having probably stayed past the end of her shift many times to check on a patient's outcome, the nurse nodded. "I understand."

"You said I had two messages?"

"The other's from Dr. Gregory Jessup. He's operating on Mr. Reynolds, but is concerned about Dr. Travis. He thinks Dr. Travis isn't feeling well and that perhaps you could check on him."

Daniel wasn't feeling well? And if he wasn't in surgery, where was he?

"Where is Dr. Travis?"

"Dr. Jessup said to go to Dr. Travis's office. He thinks you'll find him there. He said that if he wasn't, to wait and he'd soon show."

"Let me tell Mrs. Reynolds where I'm going, then I'll be on my way." She paused, remembering the security panel. "Only I won't be able to get to Daniel's office.

I'm with Cardico and only here for the week. I don't have an access code."

The nurse smiled and held up a piece of paper. "Dr. Jessup said to give you these numbers." She practically sighed with pleasure before elaborating. "He whispered them in my ear. They're his security clearance code and he didn't trust anyone else to hear them."

She looked in heaven that Gregory had given her the number and Kimberly suspected Gregory would be getting the pretty nurse's number before the night ended.

Kimberly took the paper, thanked the woman and headed to Daniel's office. She'd been there often enough during the week to find her way without any difficulties, but when she stood outside the door she found herself at a loss. She couldn't bear it if Daniel turned her away.

Was she ever going to stop being a coward when it came to Daniel?

She put her hand on the doorknob. She didn't really expect the handle to turn, because Daniel's office would be locked, right? But it turned, and she had no choice but to push the door open.

Daniel sat at his desk with his eyes closed.

"You got through a lot quicker than I was expecting," he said without opening his eyes. "Did you lose him?"

He thought she was someone else. Gregory, from the sound of it.

"Daniel?"

His eyes popped open. They were bloodshot.

As if from crying.

A strangled sound erupted from deep within him and she covered her mouth.

"What are you doing here?" He glared at her with the

hatred she'd seen earlier. And anger. Anger poured off him. "I sent a message for you to go home."

"I'm not leaving you." Running away would be much easier than facing him, but she couldn't leave. Not when she sensed he needed her more at this moment than he ever had.

His jaw tensed. "I'm not in the mood, Kimberly. Finding out I have a fourteen-year-old son has given me a lot to think about, and I want to be alone."

"No."

A blond brow quirked. "No?"

"I told you, I'm not leaving you."

He laughed, an embittered chuckle that erupted from deep within his chest. "Oh, you'll leave all right. Come tomorrow you'll hop on that plane and you'll go back to Atlanta and push me out of your mind, just as you've always done."

"It's not like that."

"Sure it is."

He attacked out of fear. She recognized all the symptoms. It was easier to attack than to admit how upset he was about Mr. Reynolds and Ryan.

Her gaze locked with his red-rimmed eyes and she crossed the room to stand next to him, turning the swivel chair to face her.

"Come with me to Atlanta, Daniel," she pleaded. She hadn't known that had been what she was going to say, but now that Daniel knew about Ryan, she wanted him to see his son, to know and love Ryan. "Come meet our son."

He swallowed, but didn't speak.

Emotion threatened to burst free. She could see the

pain spilling from his every pore. Yet he remained impassive, remained tersely silent, holding in all his hurt.

Not caring that she bared her soul, she knelt before him, took his hands and pulled them to her heart. "I'm sorry, Daniel. So very sorry. All I've ever wanted was to love you, and I know I hurt you but, please, try to understand how I felt when I found out I was pregnant. I made a mistake in not telling you, but I was trying to let you live your dream."

His eyes searched hers and something visibly crumbled inside him. Something fierce and more powerful than a dam bursting and unleashing tumultuous waters.

He leaned forward, resting against her, and she immediately wrapped her arms around him, holding him, offering comfort however she could.

Although she wasn't consciously aware of him sliding out of his chair, he must have done so because he knelt with her, tightly bound in her arms.

His body shook, and she realized he was crying, and that he didn't want her to know he was crying. Helplessness washed over her.

She'd do anything, give anything, to ease his suffering.

He mumbled something low, but it was muffled against her neck and she only caught "He died." At least, that's what she thought he'd said.

Deciding he must be speaking about Mr. Reynolds, rather than Ryan, she snuggled closer. Daniel's heart had been wrenched too many times tonight.

"Daniel," she whispered, holding him as near to her heart as she could, dropping kisses of comfort on his neck. "You did all you could."

"But he died."

"No, Mr. Reynolds is still in surgery with Gregory. He's going to be okay." In her heart, she knew the man had to be. Daniel needed him to be.

"My dad."

Two words that leveled her.

She pressed more kisses to his neck, pulling back, kissing his cheek. "Daniel, your father died because of a resistant Staphylococcus infection. Not because of anything you did."

She wasn't sure he heard her or, if he did, that her words registered.

"I was with him when he died. I tried to save him, but he died anyway."

She pulled back, cupped Daniel's face, and held his gaze. "His body was under too much strain from the infection, Daniel. His death wasn't anyone's fault, least of all yours."

"In my head, I know you're right, but in my heart..." He stopped, closed his eyes and winced.

In his heart he ached, had for years, and Ken Reynolds's little boy had slapped Daniel in the face with the past when his defenses had already been overwhelmed.

Not knowing what to say to take away his pain, but needing to lighten his burden, Kimberly leaned forward and kissed him. A soft kiss meant to lift his sorrows, to take them on herself, and give him strength.

She tasted his salty tears and kissed him again, licking away all traces of his pain. She kissed him again and again. Each time with more and more passion.

Her hands dropped and gripped his shoulders, curling into the muscles beneath her fingertips. Her heart blossomed beneath Daniel's tears and touch.

"What are you doing, Kimberly?" he asked hoarsely.

"What I've wanted to do for so long. So very, very long." She kissed him again. On the mouth. Hard. With all her longing unleashed in the way she kissed him, touched him.

"Let me love you, Daniel."

His arms around her, Daniel stood, lifting her with him. He carried her to the sofa and together they sank onto the buttery softness.

"You're playing with fire, Kimberly," he warned. "I'm not thinking straight, but I know we shouldn't be doing this. Not here. Not now. Not after what you told me."

"Yes, Daniel, we should." Not wanting him to argue with her, she covered his mouth in another kiss. One meant to shut him up.

Because, whatever the consequences, the look in Daniel's eyes no longer shone with hurt but hunger instead.

Hot, juicy hunger.

And although making love had been the last thing on her mind when she'd entered his office, her body always responded to Daniel's nearness and seemed ready, willing and able to comfort him in any way he'd let her.

Hadn't he said her body had told him all he'd needed to know the night before?

If she couldn't tell him how much she loved him, she'd at least show him.

What had he done? Daniel wondered twenty minutes later. Fool. Fool. Fool.

At the restaurant, before all hell had broken lose, he'd meant to take her back to her hotel room, strip her naked and refresh his memory.

But she'd told him about Ryan.

A son he hadn't known he had, and he'd contemplated taking her back to the hotel and wrapping his hands around her pretty little neck instead.

Then Ken Reynolds had suffered a myocardial infarction in the restaurant and his own needs had become secondary.

Instead of a night of leisurely making love to a woman he'd always wanted, or even a night of making her tell him everything there was to know about a child he hadn't known he'd had, his world had crumbled. And he'd taken her on his office sofa.

What kind of cheap Lothario would she think him?

Then again, she'd thought so little of him that she'd kept knowledge of his son from him, so what did it matter? She hadn't trusted him to do the right thing and in the end she'd destroyed his trust in her and the way she made him feel.

What they had was cheap.

They hadn't even undressed.

Daniel pulled away from her, went to toss away his condom, and realized he hadn't worn one.

"Hell."

Kimberly's eyes opened. "Daniel?"

"I didn't use a condom."

Her troubled gaze met his and she softly smiled. "It's okay, Daniel. What's the likelihood of you making me pregnant the only time we've had sex without a condom?"

"Apparently I made you pregnant *with* a condom, so you tell me," he said, doing up his jeans.

"It's the wrong time of the month." But she looked away, making him wonder if she was telling the truth.

Then again, he might just be suspicious because she'd lied to him for half of her life. Lied and cheated him of his son.

"Good." The last thing they needed was for her to get pregnant again before they resolved the issues between them.

Which drew him up short.

Was that what he wanted? To resolve the issues between them? And if so, resolve them to what end?

At the moment he hated her, yet he'd carried her to the sofa and buried his sorrows in her delectable body with little hesitation.

Because he'd wanted her, had thought they had a chance of starting over, had believed in what was between them.

Nothing but lies was between them.

Lies and a teenage son.

"Why did you just have sex with me?"

She blinked startled green eyes. "What do you mean?"

"I mean, why did we just have sex on my office sofa?"

Her cheeks pink, she sat up and straightened her clothing. "What kind of question is that, Daniel?"

"One I'd like an answer to."

She sighed, then looked at him. Sadness touched her eyes as she reached out to caress his face. "Please, don't tear apart what we just shared or ask me to explain what I don't understand myself."

CHAPTER TWELVE

KIMBERLY knew the consequences of having unprotected sex.

Yet she'd welcomed Daniel into her arms without any thought of protection.

She was a nurse, for goodness' sake. She knew the risks, knew all the reasons to use a barrier, yet she'd just lost herself in giving herself to Daniel, in easing his heartache. And pleasure—she'd lost herself in that, too.

She'd been totally irresponsible.

"What we just shared?" Daniel snorted, doing up his pants. "We had sex on my office sofa like a couple of teenagers."

Blood rushed to her face and she tired of holding in her feelings for him. She steeled herself to exposing her heart.

"I made love to you, Daniel, because I love you."

He snorted again. Louder than before.

"I've never stopped loving you," she continued.

He rolled his eyes, clearly not believing her.

"I always will love you."

"A man could do without your kind of love."

"I was scared, Daniel, little more than a child

myself. If you can't understand my fear, that's your problem."

"I can't believe you didn't call me to tell me, Kimberly." He grimaced. "Did you think I'd turn my back on you to punish you for breaking up with me?"

She averted her eyes, felt his gaze burning into her.

"You knew?" The two words came out in a horrified accusation. "You knew you were pregnant when you broke things off with me?" He paused. "You would have been around four or five months pregnant when I came home that Christmas. *You knew?*"

"I knew," she admitted unnecessarily.

"And you didn't tell me? You pushed me out of your life for some other man, knowing that my baby grew inside you?"

"There was no other man and you have no idea what it was like to be seventeen, pregnant and a thousand miles away from the person you most needed at your side."

"All you had to do was tell me and I'd have been on a plane home."

"Which was exactly why I couldn't tell you. Why I had to break things off between us."

"What the hell is that supposed to mean?"

"That you needed to finish school."

"I could have done that with you by my side."

"And lost your scholarship."

"I'd have figured something out."

"I didn't want you to have to figure something out. I wanted you to have your dream."

He took his time answering, which made her wonder if she was getting through to him.

"What about your dreams, Kimberly?"

A small smile lifted her lips. "You were my dream, Daniel. The only one that ever mattered, until Ryan came along. Any time I got discouraged at the craziness of having a baby, going to school and working, I thought of you. It gave me strength to do what needed to be done."

"I should have been with you."

"You were needed here. Saving lives and making a difference in the world."

"A difference in the world? Do you think that's important when my own son doesn't know me?"

"You'd have hated me for stealing your dream."

"I'd have found new dreams."

"No, you wouldn't have." She remained adamant. "Not on this."

He leaned back against the sofa, raked a hand through his hair. "You have no idea what you're talking about."

"You needed to do this because of your father, Daniel. Don't deny it because we both know it's true."

"My father?" He frowned. "He has nothing to do with why you didn't tell me I had a son."

"Doesn't he?" She bit her tongue. Dragging Leona into this would just be wrong.

"What does that mean?"

"I know about your father, Daniel. That you were the one who found him, that you blamed yourself, and that's why you wanted to go into cardiology. I know that."

"You know nothing."

"I know every time you operate on someone you're battling to save your father."

"That's the most ridiculous thing I've ever heard. You're trying to distract me from the facts here. The facts being that you deceived me and stole my son."

"I didn't steal Ryan. You gave him to me of your own free will."

"Oh, is that how a judge will see it?"

"A judge?" Now she was the one who sounded horrified. "You're going to seek custody?"

"What would you do if you were in my shoes?"

She'd want to get to know her son. She couldn't blame him for wanting the same. But custody?

She struggled for breath. "You could visit us in Atlanta."

"Visit?" His brow lifted. "I have fourteen years to make up for. Visiting isn't going to cut it."

"It's the best I can offer."

"Hardly. You could ask for a transfer to Boston. If Cardico's crazy enough to lose you, you could work on the cardiology floor here."

"Transfer?" Her mind reeled from the implications of what he was saying. "I can't transfer."

"Why not?"

"Ryan loves his school. Moving would mean leaving his friends, his sports teams." She met his gaze. She'd better let him know right now that usurping Ryan's life for his convenience wasn't an option. Not any more than discovering his father would already do. "I won't turn Ryan's life upside down, Daniel."

"You already have, Kimberly. You cheated him out of knowing me, out of having a father. Does he even know I'm alive?"

"Yes."

"Yes?" He sounded surprised. "What does he know?"

"That I got pregnant by my high school sweetheart. I told him you were a good man, but things didn't work out."

"So he thinks I just left him?"

"No." She shook her head. "He knows you had other commitments."

"Other commitments? What's that supposed to mean?"

"University."

"He thinks I abandoned him to go to college?"

"No." She shook her head, wincing. "We don't talk about this, Daniel. We haven't for years and years. When he was small he asked me about his father and I told him you were a good man, but had other commitments. He's never asked about you since."

Daniel winced. "He thinks I'm a jerk who walked out on a woman he made pregnant."

"No, he doesn't."

He grabbed her arms. "How do you know that if you haven't talked with him about me in years?"

Good point. "I just know." But did she? She and Ryan hadn't talked about Daniel since he'd been in kindergarten. For that matter, why hadn't her son asked more questions? She'd always expected him to but had counted herself fortunate not to have to field her son's curiosity about his father.

"You know nothing."

A loud knock on Daniel's office door had Kimberly jumping, but Daniel seemed unmoved. His hands still clutched her arms.

"Daniel?" Gregory called.

"Go away," Daniel ordered, his angry eyes not leaving her.

The door handle turned and Gregory stepped in un-invited. "I didn't realize you had company."

But Gregory didn't leave, just stared at them. Worry filled his eyes. "Hey, man, what's going on?"

"I'll tell you later."

Gregory's gaze dropped to where Daniel's fingers were digging into Kimberly's arms. Daniel didn't let go and sent his friend a warning look.

"You okay?" Gregory addressed Kimberly, looking back and forth between them.

She shook her head. She wasn't okay and Daniel's fingers were starting to bite into her flesh.

"Daniel? What's going on?"

Daniel's hands dropped to his sides. "Was there something in particular you wanted?"

Gregory hesitated a moment. He sighed, looked defeated at the news he'd come to deliver. "Ken Reynolds crashed on the operating table. I tried everything I knew to do, but I couldn't bring him back."

Weary with fatigue, Kimberly made her way to the cardiac lab.

Nervous flutters made her feel nauseous.

How would Daniel react to seeing her this morning? He'd disappeared while she'd sat in the waiting room, waiting with Beverly and Devon for their family to arrive to take them home.

She'd cried until she'd had no more tears to cry as she'd held the sobbing woman. When Beverly had gone into hysterics and Kimberly and one of the nurses had insisted she go to the emergency room, Kimberly had sat with Devon. When he'd woken up, she'd taken him to his mother and stayed until Beverly's parents had arrived.

She hadn't seen Daniel since he'd let go of her arms and she'd rushed to find Beverly. Gregory had stayed with Daniel in his office. When Kimberly had returned much later, they'd both left.

Daniel. Daniel. Daniel.

Part of her felt relief that he finally knew everything about Ryan and the way she felt about *him*.

Not that he'd acknowledged her love, but having told him everything in her heart made her feel freer than she had in years.

She'd been meeting Daniel each morning outside his cardiology clinic, waiting with Trina until Daniel arrived. With it being Saturday, the clinic was closed and she made her way to the women employees' locker room on the cardiac floor and changed into hospital scrubs. She'd go straight to the cardiac lab.

She would have loved the opportunity to talk with Daniel last night after consoling Mrs. Reynolds, but maybe he'd needed time alone to think about the things she'd told him. Perhaps that's why he hadn't joined them in the waiting room, as she'd expected him to do eventually.

Although she suspected it had had more to do with facing Devon Reynolds's grief.

Kimberly went to the cardiac lab, but found the room empty.

Going to the closest nurses' station, she offered a small smile.

"Can you tell me if Dr. Travis's procedures for this morning have been relocated?"

The nurse gave a surprised look. "Dr. Travis has already left for the day."

Kimberly glanced at her watch. Eight forty-five. The first procedure was scheduled for nine.

"Already left? The pacemaker placements were canceled?"

"No, Dr. Travis bumped up the schedule. He finished the last patient this morning at seven."

He'd already finished? "He'll be by later to discharge the patients, then?"

"Actually, he mentioned that Dr. Jessup would be covering for him for the rest of the day and would come by this afternoon to discharge the two patients who'll be going home. Mrs. Johnson will be staying overnight for observation."

Kimberly took a deep breath. "So Dr. Travis won't be back at the hospital today?"

The nurse shook her head. "Not that I know of."

And *she* was leaving this afternoon.

That's when Kimberly remembered just how little she knew about Daniel's life.

She didn't have his home number, didn't have his address. Nothing.

"I know you've seen me in here with Dr. Travis this week. I work at Cardico and will be leaving this afternoon. Is it possible for you to have Dr. Travis paged for me?"

The nurse looked undecided. "Is it an emergency? I'm really not supposed to."

"You can't page him unless it's an emergency?"

"No."

"Then, yes, it's an emergency."

Kimberly stood at the counter, waiting for Daniel

to respond to his page. When the phone rang, her stomach jumped.

The nurse answered, explained to Daniel why she'd called. Her eyes cut to Kimberly, her cheeks reddened, and she hung up. "He doesn't want to talk to you."

Kimberly's mouth dropped open.

"He said that if you needed anything related to Cardico for you to have Dr. Jessup paged."

"Page him." If Gregory was covering for Daniel, he might be somewhere in the hospital.

"Are you sure?" The nurse didn't appear to want to page Gregory. "Dr. Travis was upset that I'd bothered him about you."

About her. The mother of his son and he wouldn't speak to her.

"I'm sure. Page him."

Before leaving the hospital, Kimberly stopped by the ICU. Peyton and Cathy Clark sat in the waiting area. Peyton was playing with a handheld video game and barely looked up when she entered the area.

"Kimberly, how nice to see you." Cathy smiled in recognition. "Have you heard the good news?"

"No." But she could definitely use some good news.

"Aaron woke up last night and asked for Peyton."

The boy glanced up at them, but went back to his game.

"That's wonderful!" Kimberly exclaimed, excited that the family had received good news.

"Apparently he thought Peyton was shot, too. He was so relieved to see him." Cathy reached over and patted her son's thigh. "Dr. Travis came by this morning and says Aaron will probably be able to transfer to a regular hospital room tomorrow. Isn't that wonderful?"

"Wonderful." Daniel had been there and she'd missed him. "I'm so happy for you."

One man had regained a bit of his life during the night and another had lost his.

"I came by to say goodbye as I go home this afternoon. I'm glad I did because I got to hear your good news."

She spoke with Cathy a few more minutes. A nurse came in to announce they could visit with Aaron as he was awake and asking for his wife and son.

Kimberly hugged Cathy goodbye, smiled at Peyton and watched them hurry to room three, where Aaron Clark was awake and waiting.

Kimberly left the hospital, going to search for Daniel so she could tell him one last time what was in her heart.

"Ryan," Kimberly greeted her son the moment she walked through the security checkpoint, thinking he'd grown a foot during the week she'd been in Boston.

She also thought he looked more like Daniel than ever.

Daniel. She had so much to tell Ryan. Yet she had no idea how she was going to tell him that she'd spent the last week with his father.

That his father knew about him and had decided to shut them out of his life.

At least that's what she had been left to assume from her conversation with Gregory. Daniel hadn't responded to any of her attempts to contact him that morning.

She'd convinced Gregory to give her Daniel's home address and phone number, but he either wasn't at home or wasn't answering his door and phone.

She engulfed all six feet one of her son in a hug, then realized he was holding flowers.

"What have you got?"

"Tyler's mom made me." He gave a dimpled grin that said otherwise. "I didn't put up too much of a fight as I figured it would win me brownie points when I start bugging you to get my driver's permit."

Kimberly laughed and hugged him again. "I missed you."

"I couldn't tell." His lips twitched in perfect imitation of Daniel.

"Oh, Ryan." Her eyes watered and she held him tight.

"Mom?" he asked when she didn't let go.

Kimberly sniffled, trying to get her act together because the Atlanta airport wasn't the place to break down and spill a fifteen-year-old secret.

"Mom?" he repeated when she still didn't let go.

Kimberly pulled back, straightened her shoulders and gave a smile that was meant to be brave but wobbled too much to win any awards. "Did I mention that I missed you?"

He gave her a funny look, the one that said he saw more than she was letting on. Then, perhaps sensing she needed it, he leaned over and kissed her cheek. "I'm glad you're home, Mom."

"Me, too, Ryan." She raised the flowers, inhaled their sweet fragrance. "Let's go get my bags. We have a lot to catch up on."

That night, Kimberly stretched out on the sofa, listening to Ryan go on and on about the things he and Tyler had done during the week.

She tried to remain focused, but her mind kept slipping back to thoughts of Daniel.

What was he doing? Was he okay? Did he really hate her so much that he hadn't been able to bear seeing her again? And what about Ryan?

He'd said he was going to seek custody.

With him refusing to see her again, did that mean he'd changed his mind? Or just that he didn't plan to see her outside the courtroom?

"Mom?"

She blinked, realizing she had no idea what Ryan had been saying.

"You okay?"

Scolding herself for her lack of concentration, she met his gaze. His intelligent eyes said he saw too much and she recalled what she'd told Cathy Clark regarding Peyton.

Not quite able to keep the sadness from her eyes, she smiled softly. "I'm sorry, Ryan. I'm fine. It's been a long week, that's all."

Ryan stared at her, fiddled with the zipper on his fleece pullover, then pinned her beneath a blue stare that was pure Daniel Travis.

"You saw him, didn't you?"

Fear crawled up Kimberly's spine. "Saw who?"

"My father."

She couldn't suppress her surprised gasp.

"Why would you ask that?" She hadn't been lying to Daniel when she'd said that Ryan had only asked about him on one occasion. That had been not long after he'd started kindergarten and had been confronted with traditional families. He'd asked about his father, wanting to know why he didn't have one.

"Grandma told me he left you to go to Boston."

Grandma? Her mother and Ryan had talked about Daniel?

"That's why you didn't want me to go with you, wasn't it? Because you were seeing him."

Ryan really was too quick on the uptake for his own good.

"You did see him, didn't you?"

"Yes," she admitted. "I didn't know you ever talked about your father with Grandma."

"We talked about a lot of stuff after she got so sick."

Near the end her mother had required twenty-four-hour care. Kimberly and Ryan had stayed the nights with her mother, but Ryan spent the late afternoons alone with his grandmother and the nurse Kimberly had hired to sit with her during work hours.

But not once had her mother mentioned telling Ryan about Daniel.

"What did she tell you?"

"That my father broke your heart and didn't deserve you."

Yes, that sounded like her mother.

"She was wrong."

Ryan's serious young face looked pinched. "You didn't love him?"

"I loved him very much, but it was *me* who didn't deserve *him*."

Her son stared at her in confusion. "You've lost me."

"Actually, it was more a case of thinking I didn't deserve him, that he deserved better than what I could ever give him." Old hurts opened and as much as she didn't want her son to see how deep her agony went, she knew the time had come for everything to come out into the open.

"I was a nobody and Daniel was everything when we were at school. Every girl wanted him to notice her. For some reason I caught his eye during his senior year. I was a year behind him and we didn't have classes together, but that didn't matter. We found a way to spend as much time together as possible." Memories flooded her mind. "I admired Daniel so much. He knew exactly what he wanted out of life. A medical degree, to work as a heart surgeon and do research. I'd never met anyone so determined to succeed." She smiled tenderly at her son. "You're a lot like him."

"Don't say that." Ryan winced, looking very much like a little boy rather than the young man he was rapidly growing up to be. "I don't want to be like him."

Kimberly flinched. "Why? He's a good man, Ryan."

"He left you."

She took Ryan's hand in hers and held it tight, searching for the right words to explain what had happened all those years ago.

"I knew all along Daniel would forget me once he left for Boston," she began. "He wrote to me, but neither of us could afford phone calls, and I grew more and more lonely."

The letters had grown further and further apart and her loneliness had dived into depression, possibly due to her pregnancy, although she hadn't known the cause at the time.

"When I started being sick all the time and losing weight, I just thought it was nerves, but it wasn't. I was pregnant."

She relived the disbelief and terror she'd felt at that time.

"I made a doctor's appointment and found out for definite a couple of weeks before Daniel was to come home for the Christmas break. I wrote him a dozen letters, telling him, but never mailed them." How many letters had she poured her heart into, only to crumple the pages and cry herself to sleep?

"I had to tell him in person. So I planned to tell him while he was home. Unfortunately while I was at the doctor's I ran into one of Daniel's mother's friends and she must have seen the guilt on my face, because Leona called me and asked me over."

"That must have been scary for you," Ryan commiserated.

"Daniel's mother never liked me. She resented me because she thought he should be spending his time on more productive things than a girl from the wrong side of town. So it really surprised me when she called. Of course, I said yes." She'd been so hopeful that Leona had wanted to make peace, possibly because of the baby. Nothing could have been further from the truth. "She laid into me for being so selfish as to get pregnant and how could I destroy Daniel's life like that?"

Kimberly closed her eyes.

"She sounds like a witch."

"No." Kimberly shook her head. Once upon a time she'd hated Leona, but she'd forgiven her long ago. "She just loved Daniel very much and wanted what was best for him."

"If you say so."

"If I'd told Daniel I was pregnant, he'd have quit

college and come home. He'd have given up everything that was important to him because that's the kind of man he is, Ryan. He'd have done the right thing, even if it hadn't been what he wanted. Leona knew that, and she'd always believed I was bad for him. My getting pregnant only confirmed her suspicions as far as she was concerned.

"When it came down to it, I wasn't what he wanted. I broke things off, telling him I'd met someone else and didn't want to wait for someone so far away. At first he looked angry and hurt, but then…" she inhaled "…he just looked relieved, and I knew Leona was right."

"Relieved?"

"Maybe he'd met someone else in Boston. Or maybe he realized how difficult it was to maintain a relationship from a thousand miles away. Or maybe he just realized that we weren't meant to be." She picked up a throw cushion and toyed with the fringe. "I'm not sure. I just know things ended that Christmas."

"He never knew about me?"

"Not until this week."

"You told him about me?" Ryan looked incredulous.

"Yes."

"What did he say?" The hopeful look in his eyes undid her.

"He's upset, Ryan."

"Upset?" He frowned. "What's that mean?"

"It means he has a life of his own and finding out he fathered a child fifteen years ago caught him off guard."

Ryan crossed his arms, flexing his young jaw. "He didn't care, did he?"

Kimberly's heart broke at the raw emotion on her son's

face. Ryan needed Daniel to care, wanted to know his father hadn't rejected him. "He cared, Ryan. A great deal."

"So where is he?" Ryan looked around as if he expected to see Daniel. "If he knows about me, and he cares so much, why isn't he here?"

"He has a busy life in Boston, Ryan." She didn't know what else to say. She wouldn't undermine Daniel. Yet she didn't understand why he hadn't made plans to meet Ryan. "There's something else I need to tell you, just in case."

Suspicion entered Ryan's eyes. "What? Does he want a paternity test or something?"

"No." Daniel had seemed to believe her when she'd told him about Ryan being his son, but she supposed asking for a paternity test wouldn't have been unreasonable of Daniel. "He says he's going to fight for custody."

Ryan's eyes widened with a mixture of relief and denial. "No way."

Kimberly nodded. "He wants to get to know you, and visiting you occasionally in Atlanta isn't enough."

"I won't go."

Kimberly nodded. "I wouldn't let him take you, Ryan, not unless it was what you wanted, but, as your father, he does have rights. Our lives may change to accommodate his place in your life."

"No, he doesn't have any rights," Ryan denied, shaking his head. "He's not a part of our lives. I don't even know him."

"Which is my fault," she admitted, hugging the pillow to her. "If I'd told Daniel about my pregnancy, you'd have grown up knowing your father."

Ryan's jaw took on a stubborn set and he took her hand in his again, squeezing it reassuringly. "I grew up just fine."

Love for her son spread through her. She'd been so blessed by having Ryan in her life. A blessing Daniel hadn't known.

"Yes, but you've missed out on things by not having your father around." She and Ryan had survived just fine, but was fine good enough when Ryan could have had better? Should have had better? "By not having Daniel in your life because he's innocent in all this, Ryan. I made the decision not to tell him about you and it's my fault you grew up without knowing your father." She sighed. "I should have told him the truth a long time ago."

They sat on the sofa, holding hands and quietly thinking about what had been said.

"I want to meet him."

Kimberly glanced at her son, not surprised by his words.

"Ryan, I…" What could she say? She didn't know Daniel's heart? But she had seen his hurt. No matter how much he hated her, he'd never turn Ryan away. "Okay."

"When?" Ever the doer, once a decision was made Ryan wanted things to happen pronto. In this case that wouldn't work. Not with school, sports, and her work.

"Spring break, while you're off school."

About six weeks away, but the best Kimberly could offer without Ryan having to miss school.

"We can't go next weekend?"

If she'd agree, Ryan would be packing their bags to head back to Boston tonight. Daniel needed time to adjust to the idea. She'd give him time to come to his senses so that when Ryan reached out to him, Daniel would be ready and Ryan wouldn't be hurt.

"What about basketball?"

Ryan's brow quirked. "What about it?"

Knowing he would persist, trying to wear her down, she changed tactics. Her son was nothing if not protective of her, and she truly couldn't face the thought of returning to Boston again so quickly.

"I'm not up to going back to Boston and seeing Daniel again. Not this soon. I'm sorry."

The truth if she'd ever spoken it, but if it had been the right thing for Ryan, she'd book their flights immediately. If only she knew what was in Daniel's head, and his heart.

Resigned to the delay, Ryan leaned back on the sofa and stared at the ceiling. "You know, I heard you that night."

Kimberly frowned. "What night?"

"The night I asked you about my father," he clarified, causing Kimberly to place her hand over her mouth in remembered shame.

"I heard you crying," he continued, "and I swore if I ever met the man who'd hurt you that much, I'd kill him."

"Ryan!"

"I talked with Grandma about it the next day and she told me not to ask you about him ever again because he'd broken your heart."

"Grandma shouldn't have told you that."

"Why not? It's true."

"I broke my own heart by being too scared to fight for what I wanted, Ryan. I wanted Daniel to fight for me, but when it came down to it, I was the one who didn't fight. I pushed him away and expected him to somehow know how much I was hurting, to know how much I needed him to need me. It wasn't his fault he couldn't read my mind or that he didn't love me back." She couldn't let Ryan place the blame on Daniel. "I didn't fight for his love and I lost it. That was my fault, not Daniel's."

And when she said the words out loud, she knew they were true.

CHAPTER THIRTEEN

A MONTH later, Kimberly sat on her sofa, working on her laptop. She'd arrived home late, but Ryan was at Tyler's. Although they'd spent the previous weekend at Tyler's, working on a global warming project, Ryan had still gone to his friend's following basketball every evening that week, perfecting the science project. No doubt the boys would get a top grade for it.

Glad it was Friday, she'd come home, heated up left-over soup, changed into her pajamas, and curled up on the sofa to get some work done. But an hour had gone by and she'd barely made a dent in her work.

Her mind kept drifting off to making love with Daniel on his office sofa and in her hotel room bed. She closed her eyes and felt his lips on hers, felt his hands on her body.

She ached. Ached deep inside at what might have been if life had played them a different hand. What would have happened if she hadn't became pregnant that summer? If they'd had the opportunity to play out their relationship?

She wouldn't have Ryan, that's what.

Nothing was worth that sacrifice.

Five weeks had gone by and she hadn't heard a peep out of Daniel.

She hadn't really expected him to change his mind about her. She hoped he'd forgive her someday, but understood why he apparently couldn't.

But she had trouble believing he'd continued to ignore Ryan.

Ignoring the fact he had a son didn't fit with what she knew about him. Daniel wouldn't neglect his child. Yet that was exactly what he was doing.

Each day that passed tore at her heart.

And Daniel's lack of interest was getting to Ryan.

Not that her son complained, but he'd asked her about Daniel repeatedly in those first few days after she'd returned home. Asking her to tell him everything about their past, everything that had happened during the week she spent in Boston.

She hadn't told him everything. But Ryan wasn't a fool and probably saw the truth on her face when she'd edited what had happened between her and Daniel.

Ryan hungered for knowledge about his father, about how she'd cared for him.

Just last week he'd asked her point blank if she loved Daniel.

Although she hadn't wanted to lay that burden on her son, she absolutely refused to lie to him. She did love Daniel and had admitted as much.

Ryan hadn't asked her about Daniel since that night, but she saw how he continued to jump when the phone rang, how he avoided her eyes at times. Like he felt guilty.

She didn't want him to feel guilty for wanting Daniel's attention and love.

Neither did she want him to get hurt if Daniel didn't react well to his son showing up on his doorstep in a week's time.

She'd call on Monday, make arrangements for Ryan to meet him, for them to spend time together. If Daniel wouldn't talk with her, she'd go through Gregory. Or Trina. Or the entire Boston Memorial Hospital staff. But she would give her son the opportunity to meet his father.

A week and she'd be back in Boston.

Face-to-face with Daniel. Because she wouldn't leave without seeing him, without him meeting Ryan, without telling him there was no need for lawyers. Ryan could spend as much time with Daniel as he wanted or Ryan liked.

Based on Ryan's interest in Daniel, she suspected that would be quite a lot.

She'd miss him, but she would encourage her son to enjoy each moment with Daniel.

Even Leona, if the woman wanted to be a part of Ryan's life. Leona was Ryan's only living grandparent. And although Leona had fertilized the seeds of doubt already in Kimberly's mind, Leona had been protecting Daniel, doing what she'd believed right for her son.

Loving Ryan the way Kimberly did and having not always made the right decisions, she could forgive Leona for that. Although she'd never understand how the woman could have wanted her to abort Daniel's baby. Still, all that was in the past and better off forgotten.

But if Daniel turned Ryan away, she'd never forgive him.

Just the thought of seeing her son hurt made her livid.

Was that yet another reason she'd delayed in telling Daniel?

She sighed. Who knew all her reasons? Over the years they'd built up and time had made ignoring what had needed to be done easier and easier. She'd been wrong not to tell Daniel. She saw that now, but she didn't regret that she'd given him the opportunity to fulfill his dream.

Only that she should have found the strength to tell him and still help him achieve his potential as a talented heart surgeon.

She heard the front door, glanced at her watch and smiled that her son had come home earlier than his ten o'clock curfew.

She'd barely seen him all week.

"I'm in here," she called, closing down her computer program so she could spend time with him. Maybe they'd play a game of chess or just watch a movie together. "Did you and Tyler finish your science project?"

Ryan spoke, but so low she couldn't understand what he'd said. Tyler must have come home with him. No problem as he was like a second son to her, but Ryan usually called to ask first. She wondered why he hadn't tonight.

The moment her son and his guest stepped into the living room, she knew why her son hadn't called.

"Daniel."

Dressed in jeans, T-shirt, and a beat-up leather jacket, Daniel looked fabulous. And he was standing in her living room next to a younger image of himself—Ryan.

Had she not been sitting down she surely would have fainted.

"Mom, I…" Ryan looked at Daniel a bit helplessly, and the understanding that passed between them spoke volumes. The weight of the moment and what their exchange meant settled on Kimberly.

Ryan had been talking with Daniel.

"How long?" she squeaked out, trying to keep the accusation from her voice, to ignore the fact she was wearing only thin cotton pajamas and Daniel's gaze was traveling over her curled-up form. Tingles of awareness pricked her skin, while anger raged inside her. She fought her reaction to Daniel, focusing on her anger to keep her pain at bay.

Ryan had every right to talk with his father, but why hadn't he told her? Irrational as her thoughts were, she felt betrayed.

"The week after you left Boston," Daniel answered, placing his hand on Ryan's shoulder as their son glanced back and forth between them.

"How?" she bit out, trying to curb her anger and betrayal for Ryan's sake.

"I called Ryan's cell phone."

"How did you get his number?"

Placing his hands in his jeans pockets, Daniel shrugged. "It's not difficult to get someone's cell number if you know who to ask."

Had someone at Cardico given him that information?

She bit her lower lip, trying to decipher what all this meant, why Daniel was standing in her living room, looking as comfortable as could be with Ryan.

"How long have you been in town?" she asked, full of suspicion.

"I flew in last Friday."

"Last Friday?" Kimberly gulped. Ryan had spent last weekend with Tyler.

Only he hadn't. He'd been with Daniel. And every night since.

Ryan had lied to her.

She turned betrayed eyes on her son. "You've not been to Tyler's at all this week, have you?"

Ryan winced, and she struggled to get her emotions under control. She'd put him in this situation, created this monstrosity that left him feeling like he couldn't be with Daniel without lying to her. She couldn't blame him for wanting to see Daniel, to spend time with his father. And yet pain sliced through her.

"Mom, I didn't want to hurt you."

"You having lied to me hurts." She reminded herself she'd set the motions into play fifteen years ago that had led to this moment, to this sense of shattered trust. "I wouldn't have stopped you from seeing Daniel."

Ryan stepped toward her, then paused. He stared at her, looking uncertain what to say, and she hated the unfamiliar awkwardness between them.

"I asked Ryan not to tell you that I'd contacted him, Kimberly."

She narrowed her gaze at Daniel and focused all her emotions into her fury at him. "You asked my son to lie to me? How dare you?"

"*Our* son," he firmly reminded her.

"Oh, and teaching him to lie to his mother is your first fatherly duty?" she lashed out. An entire week. No wonder Ryan hadn't been able to look her in the eye.

"Ryan." Daniel turned to the younger version of himself and placed a comforting hand on Ryan's shoulder again. "Perhaps you should go to your room so your mother and I can talk."

Ryan hesitated, and Daniel gave him a pointed look. "Go."

Ryan still didn't budge, his eyes lingering on Kimberly. Knowing the dam within her was readying to burst, she nodded. She didn't want Ryan to see her tears.

Neither did she want to say something hurtful in anger. None of this was Ryan's fault. Even through her hurt and fury she recognized she could only blame herself.

And Daniel. She blamed him, too. He should have called her, told her he wanted to see Ryan.

"You're sure?" Ryan apparently didn't want to leave her alone with Daniel. His eyes had taken on a defensive look and she knew he was battling with his budding emotions for his father and his sense of loyalty to her. She didn't want this to be any harder for Ryan than it already was.

"Daniel's right. We need to talk, and it would be best for that conversation to be in private."

Ryan exchanged a look with Daniel, then nodded at Kimberly. "I'll be upstairs if you need me."

Her heart clenched at the protectiveness in his tone. Whatever had passed between Daniel and himself, Ryan was making it clear that he didn't want her hurt. Which was all the more reason for him not to witness how deep her pain ran where Daniel was concerned.

The moment his bedroom door closed, his stereo came on, loud.

Hating that she was wearing worn cotton pajamas, Kimberly stood up and rounded on Daniel. She couldn't stand having to look so far up at him.

"How dare you have my son deceive me?"

Daniel's gaze didn't waver, neither did he have the decency to look ashamed. "We needed time to get to know each other without you in the middle."

"Without…" She stopped, his meaning slamming home. He'd come for Ryan. She narrowed her gaze, wondering how such a brilliant man could be so dense. "I wouldn't have told you about Ryan if I was going to keep him away from you."

"Not for the first time, you're jumping to the wrong conclusion." Daniel took a step toward her. "He and I needed time to work out our relationship on our own. Without meaning to, you would have impeded that."

His words slapped her in the face. He didn't trust her to not stand in the way of he and Ryan developing a relationship.

"No," she denied, but perhaps he was right. She would have worried about Ryan getting hurt. She might have been overly protective and in some way delayed their bonding.

Daniel stood at the side of the living room, watching her, making her more self-conscious about the faded red pajamas Ryan had given her for Christmas a couple of years back.

Moments passed, marked only by the clicking of the mantel clock and the music from Ryan's room.

Unable to stand the silence and his searching blue gaze, she put her hands on her hips, mostly because she needed to do something with them.

"If you expect me to say I agree with you sneaking around behind my back…" she glared "…you're sadly mistaken. You should have told me."

"Like you told me?" His accusation stung.

"That's different."

"Is it?" he asked, slowly crossing the room with confident strides. When he stood a foot from her, he stopped and stared down at her. "Tell me, Kimberly, how is it different?"

"Because I did it for you."

He stood too close, and she couldn't meet his eyes. Lowering her gaze only meant staring at the way he filled out his leather jacket.

"Did you?"

She glanced up, all the realizations she'd made since first seeing him in the cardiac lab the morning he'd put in Ellen Mills's pacemaker hitting her full force.

"At first." Kimberly swallowed, feeling weak and on the verge of tears. How could she be so angry and yet want to weep with great sadness at the same time?

"And then, later, when keeping your secret wasn't doing it for me?" His eyes searched hers, and when she looked away he lifted her chin, forcing her to meet his eyes. "Tell me."

Her flesh burned from the heat of his touch and she hated the power he held over her body. Over her heart.

"I was afraid."

"Of me?"

"Of everything," she cried, no longer restraining the fat, wet teardrops rolling down her cheeks. "Of the fact I'd made a mistake. Of realizing you'd moved on with your life. Of the fact you'd hate me when I told you I'd kept him from you."

"I did hate you," he admitted, confirming what she already knew.

A sob escaped her lips and she wished he'd let her face go so she could look away, hide her hurt.

"But then…" his eyes held hers and his thumb caressed her chin "…I forgave you."

"You did?" Dare she believe that he might really forgive her? That they could find some sort of peace for Ryan?

"No matter how much I hurt that I've missed out on knowing my son, I hurt more because I let you go through this alone."

"You didn't know I was pregnant."

"But I should have." He took a deep breath, cupped her face. "Tell me, Kimberly. If I'd pushed you, would you have told me the truth that Christmas?"

"About being pregnant?"

"Yes."

Would she have? She'd wanted nothing more than for Daniel to take her in his arms and insist he was never letting her go. What if he had? Would she have broken down and told him everything? Or would guilt at stealing his dream have kept her lips sealed?

"I don't know," she admitted.

"I made it easy for you to believe you were making the right choice. I walked away without fighting for you."

In her heart, she had expected Daniel to refuse to let her end their relationship. To demand she tell him what was going on and why she would say such a foolish thing. She'd expected him to see through her lies and know she had felt shattered on the inside and had needed him.

He hadn't. He'd been angry, but he'd agreed. No more fuss. No more bother.

"You left because you had to return to school." She told him what she'd told herself for fifteen years.

"I left because leaving was easier than staying to fight for you."

She wobbled slightly toward him. "I don't understand."

"I was scared of how much you meant to me, how much I wanted to come home to be with you." He gave a self-derisive laugh. "I spent my first semester busting my gut, learning everything I could, but you distracted me at every turn."

"I was a thousand miles away."

"Didn't matter if you'd been on the other side of the earth, Kimberly. You distracted me."

"Oh."

"I missed you so much all I could think about was coming home to you at Christmas. When you told me you'd met someone else, I was angry at you. I'd been lying awake at night, dreaming of you, and you'd been out with some other guy."

"There wasn't anyone else, Daniel."

"I know that. Now. But I didn't then and I wanted to hate you for tossing my love aside. I didn't want you to see how I hurt. And, truth be told, I realized finishing medical school wasn't going to happen if you were in my life, because knowing you were in Atlanta, waiting for me, just made me want to pack up and come home."

Somehow, hearing him confirm all her suspicions didn't ease her heart the way she'd expected.

"When I broke up with you, you were glad?"

"Not glad, but relieved because I felt disloyal to my father's memory every time I thought about quitting."

"Because of what happened to him? His death wasn't your fault, Daniel."

"No, but for twenty-five years I've blamed myself, and my mother let me."

"Leona? I don't understand."

"She and I had quite a discussion last weekend after I took Ryan to meet her."

"Ryan met Leona?" Kimberly swayed. She only kept from sagging onto the sofa behind her because Daniel's hands grabbed her arms and held her.

"Yes. She was shocked to see him walk into her house." The warmth of his hands burned through her pajama top, searing her arms. "But not as shocked as she should have been."

Thoughts of Leona meeting Ryan caused Kimberly to wince. Poor Ryan. Though he must have done fine, she wanted to rush the stairs and take him in her arms, demand to know what Leona had said to him, if she'd been cruel or hateful.

"She told me everything."

Once again Kimberly wobbled. "Everything?"

A sick look crossing his face, Daniel nodded. "She admitted she tried to convince you to have an abortion and she's struggled with her conscience ever since. She thought you had done so until she read your mother's obituary."

Kimberly tried to digest what Daniel was saying. Leona regretted the things she'd said that afternoon?

"Daniel, I never considered abortion as an option for our baby."

"Thank God," he said emphatically. "I want to be angry at her for her role in this, just as I'd wanted to hang on to my anger at you." He brushed his palms down her arms in a slow caress and linked their fingers. "Blaming everyone else is easier than taking the blame myself, but I'd already realized my guilt. No matter what my mother had said or done, if I'd fought for you, Ryan would have grown up with a mother and a father."

Daniel was taking the blame?

Staring at their twined hands and wondering at the meaning of his embrace, Kimberly tried to digest all the things Daniel had said. "Your mother accepted Ryan as your son?"

"How could she not?" Daniel's gaze landed on a framed photo of Ryan on the coffee table beside them. "Like you once said, he's my image."

There was no denying Ryan's genetic heritage.

"I'd agree to a paternity test, if you want one."

"There's no need." He shook his head. "I never doubted you, but if I had, from the moment I first spoke with him I knew he was mine."

Kimberly's heart constricted at the possessiveness in Daniel's voice.

"When I met him last Friday…" He paused, his voice choked with emotion. "My whole life had been leading up to that moment."

Kimberly nodded, recalling how she'd felt the first time she'd held her newborn son in her arms, looked into his face and known he was her greatest accomplishment. She still got that feeling when looking at Ryan.

"For the record, Mom accepted Ryan as mine from the moment she read the obituary and saw you had a son."

"What do you mean?"

"After Ryan went to bed—we stayed at her place on Friday night—she pulled out an album full of clippings about Ryan. She said she even got the nerve to go to one of his games this fall. After the game was when she started pushing for me to move home."

"Because she wanted to tell you about Ryan?"

"No, she didn't have the nerve because she blamed herself for me not knowing about Ryan. She blamed herself for you dumping me and keeping Ryan from me. I'm all she has left and she couldn't bear the thought of losing me over her mistake, so she kept quiet, hoping I'd move back and somehow discover my son."

The weight of what Leona must have gone through crushed any remaining negative feelings Kimberly had toward Daniel's mother. If only Leona had come to her, she would have welcomed her into Ryan's life. After all, Ryan hadn't any other grandparents.

"She only said what I was already thinking," Kimberly admitted, dizzy at all the pain that touched their lives because of actions taken so long ago. "I don't blame her for what happened."

"You blame me?"

"No." But that wasn't entirely true, so she backed up. "I do, but mostly I blame us both, Daniel." Sadness at what might have been but would never be swept through her, leaving her bone-weary and her knees liquid. "We didn't believe in each other enough to trust our hearts. That's what ended our relationship."

"And now?"

"Now?" She shrugged, pulling her hands free from Daniel's because she couldn't bear touching him. Not when he didn't love her. "I won't interfere with you spending time with Ryan. I'll miss him while he's with you, but I'll encourage him to spend his summers in Boston."

Daniel's forehead wrinkled, and he refused to let her pull her hands away. "Why in Boston?"

Biting her lower lip, she fought the urge to demand he quit torturing her with his tender touch. "Because it's where you live."

He shook his head. "Ryan won't be spending his summers in Boston."

Did he expect Ryan to move with him immediately and to spend his summers in Atlanta? How would she bear being away from him so long?

"I turned my notice in the day after I spoke with Ryan. I've spent the last month tying up loose ends on the CRT and fulfilling my obligations to the university and the hospital."

Kimberly's stomach flip-flopped. "Why?"

"Because my heart's in Atlanta."

"Ryan?"

He nodded, lifting her hand to gently stroke across his cheek. "And you."

"Me?" Dare she hope?

He kissed her fingers, closed his eyes, and his throat worked.

She could dare. Hope surged through her heart.

"I want to start over, Kimberly. To finish what we started fifteen years ago."

"You want to date me?"

"I want to marry you."

* * *

Daniel waited for Kimberly to say something. Her face had gone pale and her lower lip quivered. Had he rushed things?

No, fifteen years too many had already passed with them being apart. He didn't want to waste another second of their lives being apart. After spending a weekend of torment, bouncing between anger, hatred, guilt, and love, he'd known what he wanted.

Kimberly. His son. A family, as he should have had and fought for when he'd been too young and stupid to do so.

Her big green eyes stared at him, making him weak-kneed, so he took her hand in his.

"Marry me, Kimberly. Let's give Ryan a family."

"You want to get married because of Ryan?" Her voice squeaked and her eyes shone brightly, as if more tears might fall at any moment.

"If that's the only reason you'll agree then yes, because of Ryan." He wanted her in his life. If Ryan was the catalyst, then so be it. With time, he'd win her heart. After all, healing hearts was his specialty and no one mattered more than Kimberly.

She didn't say anything, just closed her eyes, and he could feel the tension building in her body as she worked up the words to deny him.

He couldn't let that happen. Not without telling her how he felt.

"But, as much as I know you love Ryan, what I want is for you to marry me because you love me. In Boston, you told me you loved me and would always love me. Has that changed?"

Her chin lifted. "You said you didn't want my kind of love."

Her eyes glittered and he fought the urge to pull her to him and kiss her into agreement, tell her everything he wanted with his mouth and body. Hadn't he done that in Boston?

"Your love is the only love I've ever wanted, Kimberly. The only love I've ever needed."

She trembled, and he clasped her hand more firmly.

"I love you, and I want to spend the rest of my life with you and Ryan."

"You love me?"

"I've always loved you."

"Daniel," she whispered. She took his face in her hands and searched his eyes.

He waited for her to say more. She didn't, just closed her eyes and leaned her forehead against his.

"Does this mean yes?" he asked, hopeful.

"Yes." Her moist eyes opened and she smiled at him. "Oh, yes."

No longer wanting or willing to restrain himself, he pulled her into his arms and kissed her until all the breath had left his body and his head spun.

"I want more babies, Kimberly. I hope that's okay."

Her mouth fell open and she stared at him with startled eyes.

"You don't?" he asked, trying not to let his disappointment show. Kimberly and Ryan would be enough, more than enough, his whole world.

"It's not that." She looked uncertain. "It's just…"

"Just what?"

She met his gaze and gave him a nervous look. "When you said more babies, I realized I haven't had a period since Boston."

She looked incredulous she hadn't realized sooner. "Since Boston?"

She nodded, watching him nervously.

Life couldn't be this good. A happy laugh bubbled out of him. "A baby would be wonderful, Kimberly. More than wonderful."

"You wouldn't mind?"

"Mind?" He grinned, happier than he'd thought he could be. "I just told you I wanted more babies."

"I might not be, Daniel. Maybe it would be better if I wasn't pregnant so we'd have time to get to know one another again."

"Either way, I'm the luckiest man in the world, Kimberly, because I'll have you and Ryan. Another baby would just be the icing on the cake."

"Really?"

"Really." He kissed her long and hard, barely recalling his son waited upstairs for news of how his proposal had gone. He couldn't make love to Kimberly on the sofa. Not right now. But soon.

"Let's go tell Ryan our news."

Kimberly's gaze grew nervous. "Do you think he'll be okay with this? We're not moving too fast?"

Daniel remembered the box in his pocket. The box he should have opened and given to her already.

He slipped his hand into his pocket and pulled out the velvet-covered box.

"As he helped me pick out your ring and coached me through how I was supposed to tell you how lost I was without you, I think Ryan will be the first to congratulate us."

When they turned to the stairs, they spotted their smiling son watching them.

When Ryan gave them a sheepish grin, they enveloped him in a group hug, the first of many such hugs for their family.

MILLS & BOON

MEDICAL™

proudly presents

Brides of Penhally Bay

Featuring Dr Nick Tremayne

A pulse-raising collection of emotional, tempting romances and heart-warming stories – devoted doctors, single fathers, Mediterranean heroes, a sheikh and his guarded heart, royal scandals and miracle babies…

Book Four

THE SURGEON'S FATHERHOOD SURPRISE

by Jennifer Taylor

on sale 7th March 2008

Celebrate 100 years of pure reading pleasure with Mills & Boon®

To mark our centenary, each month we're publishing a special 100th Birthday Edition. These celebratory editions are packed with extra features and include a FREE bonus story.

Now that's worth celebrating!

4th January 2008

The Vanishing Viscountess by Diane Gaston
With FREE story The Mysterious Miss M
This award-winning tale of the Regency Underworld launched Diane Gaston's writing career.

1st February 2008

Cattle Rancher, Secret Son by Margaret Way
With FREE story His Heiress Wife
Margaret Way excels at rugged Outback heroes…

15th February 2008

Raintree: Inferno by Linda Howard
With FREE story Loving Evangeline
A double dose of Linda Howard's heady mix of passion and adventure.

Don't miss out! From February you'll have the chance to enter our fabulous monthly prize draw. See special 100th Birthday Editions for details.

www.millsandboon.co.uk

0108/CENTENARY_2-IN-1

FREE

4 BOOKS AND A SURPRISE GIFT!

We would like to take this opportunity to thank you for reading this Mills & Boon® book by offering you the chance to take FOUR more specially selected titles from the Medical™ series absolutely FREE! We're also making this offer to introduce you to the benefits of the Mills & Boon® Reader Service™—

★ FREE home delivery
★ FREE gifts and competitions
★ FREE monthly Newsletter
★ Books available before they're in the shops
★ Exclusive Reader Service offers

Accepting these FREE books and gift places you under no obligation to buy; you may cancel at any time, even after receiving your free shipment. Simply complete your details below and return the entire page to the address below. You don't even need a stamp!

YES! Please send me 4 free Medical books and a surprise gift. I understand that unless you hear from me, I will receive 6 superb new titles every month for just £2.89 each, postage and packing free. I am under no obligation to purchase any books and may cancel my subscription at any time. The free books and gift will be mine to keep in any case.

M8ZEE

Ms/Mrs/Miss/Mr...Initials ....
BLOCK CAPITALS PLEASE

Surname ....

Address ....

....

....Postcode ....

Send this whole page to:
The Reader Service, FREEPOST CN81, Croydon, CR9 3WZ